TALES OF THE BRIGHT, THE DARK, & THE BIZARRE

AUTHOR MAURICE CONNOLLY has previously been a pub landlord, an auctioneer and a farmer. He spent his early years at Kilmeaden, County Waterford, growing up on a farm with one brother, Michael. After finishing school, he worked for a spell in London, and on his return to the farm he wrote a play, *Ebbtide*, which was staged at various venues throughout the country including Dublin and Cork. Two years later he penned his second play, *Weekend Appointment*. He has also written a novel, *Redferne*.

Maurice Connolly lives in Foulksmills, County Wexford with his wife Anne. They have two sons, John and Thomas, and four grandchildren Fionn, Jack, Caoime and Charlie.

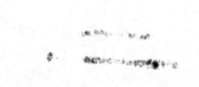

Maurice Connolly
Tales of the Bright, the Dark, & the Bizarre

SilverWood

Also by this author
Redferne

Published in paperback by SilverWood Books 2010
www.silverwoodbooks.co.uk

ISBN 978-1-906236-44-1

British Library Cataloguing in Publication Data
A CIP catalogue record for this book is available from the British Library

Set in Palatino Light by SilverWood Books
Printed in England on paper certified as being from sustainable sources

*This book is dedicated to
all those who have reached seventy years
and are looking forward to the next thirty at least*

Contents

The Battle of the Boyne, Part Two

The Donovan homestead could be classified as of medium size. The only downside being that the fields were pretty scattered—most of the land encircled the house and farmyard but a few fields were down a narrow laneway, roughly a half mile from the house.

It was at this farthest away point that young Matt found himself, walking amongst the cattle. It was a beautiful summer's day, with only the sheen of a light breeze that felt warm against his face. This was a chore he was given by his father, to go over every day during the summer holidays and count the sixteen Hereford bullocks, to walk them about, to establish if any one was lame or, generally speaking, not looking right. Young and all as Matt was—having just celebrated his twelfth birthday—his father knew he had a keen eye around livestock.

Satisfied that all was well he sat down on a clump of grass, just watching the animals grazing. He was fond of those harmless creatures. Jimmy his black and brown mongrel-type collie dog—his ever faithful companion—with tongue lolling, panting from the heat of the sun, also stretched himself out on the grass. Everything on God's earth felt so peaceful. It was great to be alive, Matt thought—apart from what was going on at home. Curious, the cattle moved ever closer, gingerly craning their necks, sniffing both dog and boy.

Feeling under threat, Jimmy suddenly leapt up, snapping, causing the cattle to jump backwards in disarray. Keeping a wary eye the dog sat back down. The cattle began to regroup. Perhaps they felt this was a type of game now—a bit of excitement, a form of diversion. Getting to his feet, glancing at his new watch, Matt decided he'd head back.

If there was one thing Matt possessed it was an extremely vivid imagination. The one and only subject he liked at school was history. In his mind's eye he re-fought all those famous battles of old. He visualized himself always in the thick of the action, always the hero to the very end, firing his pistol or flailing with his sword, saving his comrades from imminent and violent death. The greatest treat in the world for Matt was to be taken to the pictures—especially if the picture happened to be a western. Randolph Scott, that cool, fearless cowboy was his favourite film star by a mile. Matt was everything and everywhere: he was at Davy Crockett's side at the Alamo; he was Wyatt Earp's friend, walking up the street together to the OK Corral; he was the Red Baron, sweeping down through the clouds—running now, arms spread out, weaving from side to side, going *ack-ack-ack!* Jimmy bounced along by his side.

He now entered the secluded overgrown lane, on his final trek towards home. He was now General Custer at the Little Big Horn. With his left hand to his mouth, in Hollywood style, he whooped like a Redskin, holding aloft an imaginary tomahawk. He halted suddenly in his tracks as he became aware of his near neighbour, standing back in the old broken gateway, smiling in his direction.

Hal Morley was the man's name. He was another landowner, living close by. He too was accompanied by his dog, Billy, a dog very similar to Matt's Jimmy. In fact, both dogs could have been from the same litter, the resemblance being so profound. If so, there was no brotherly love apparent, as both dogs growled their displeasure at this sudden, unexpected confrontation.

Hal Morley, in his mid-fifties, seemed hewn from the rough terrain in which he lived. His face was lined, creased and weathered from the harsh outdoors, where out of necessity he spent most of his days. He hadn't shaved for several days, his clothes were threadbare and shiny from constant wear, he had strong boots on and a cap perched jauntily on his head.

Initially taken aback, Matt involuntarily experienced a sudden surge of trepidation. His mother's warning flashed into his mind: *don't ever be in a lonely place with a strange man—or with any man. Do you hear me? Do you hear me?* she'd loudly repeated. She had tears in her eyes as she shook his shoulders. *Run away as fast as your two legs will carry you,* adding, as she turned away, *what kind of a cruel world is this at all?*

This was definitely a lonely spot, Matt surmised, glancing about, as bramble, ash, blackthorn and ivy yawned inwards from both sides like withered arms reaching out to embrace him. A small stream, now reduced to a trickle, eddied down one side of the laneway. But he couldn't run away now—this was Mister Morley after all, his neighbour. What would the man think if he turned on his heels now and bolted?

"Well hallo young Donovan, and how are you this fine day?" he greeted Matt.

"I'm fine, Mister Morley."

"I was just going to grab my rifle and circle the wagons, as I was sure the injuns were on the warpath again," he smiled.

Matt smiled back sheepishly. He liked Hal Morley. There was something about Hal Morley that fascinated him. Was it the way he focused his complete attention on your every word, even when speaking to someone young like himself? Other adults might appear disinterested and indifferent. Even his own mother often dismissed him with, *shut up will you, and don't be talking nonsense.* Hal Morley was different though. Definitely different. Thinking of his mother again, a slight pang of fear re-surfaced. But what was he to be fearful of? Nothing. He noticed Jimmy's and Billy's guttural growls growing louder.

"Them two dogs would love to tear into each other." Hal commented.

"They look alike, don't they?" Matt opinionated.

Hal took a lead out of his pocket and clasped it on Billy's collar. "I'll tie this fella to the gate for a minute. Oh they look alike all right. They have the same markings. There's a family connection there no doubt. Look at them—they'd like to be tearing strips off each other."

Matt was aware that when Hal started off on a topic he'd keep on and on. He didn't mind though, because he liked the sound of Hal's voice. It had a soothing, mesmerizing effect on him, for some reason.

"But then dogs can be vicious creatures," Hal continued. "They're killers you see—they're bred to kill, it's in their nature."

"Hardly all dogs, Mister Morley?"

"Don't call me *Mister*. Nobody calls me *Mister*. Call me Hal—that's what everybody calls me."

"All right Mister Mor—I mean Hal."

"Dogs belong to the same family as wolves, you see. The wolves of the Yellowstone National Park, or the wild

14

hunting dogs of the African savannah. A dog's loyalty is what sets him apart. That's why he's called man's best friend. Aye, loyalty, you can't beat it."

"That's what I mean. I love dogs," Matt asserted.

"Did you ever hear of the black hound that was seen in this parish years ago?"

"No, never heard anything about that."

People, in general, knew that Hal was renowned as an inveterate raconteur of mind boggling tales. What with all his ghost stories and such like. Still, people enjoyed listening to his lofty flights of the imagination. Maybe it was the way he put those stories across—with the conviction and certainty he engendered.

"You were too young, too young," he continued. "Some terrible, horrible things happened, back around the time of the Civil War. Atrocious, unspeakable crimes. Some unfortunate people were dragged screaming out of their houses in the middle of the night and shot dead without pity. Shot dead without mercy, in cold blood. All sides were responsible. It was as if people had turned their backs on God—turned their backs on everything that was good and decent. When that happens evil takes over, takes control." He stared Matt straight in the face, speaking in a loud whisper: "Evil walked the earth back then. And when one of those evil men died, or was killed, the black hound was seen—always on the road near the churchyard."

Matt's eyes opened wide and he bit his lower lip. "The black hound!" he whispered, in awe.

"A nightmarish sight, with froth on its mouth and fangs *that* long," holding out two fingers. "And two eyes like burning coals. It wasn't a hound at all you see—it was the devil from hell."

"The devil!" Matt gasped.

"Oh yes, Satan himself, coming from the hobs of hell to claim one of his own."

"He's not seen now, is he?"

"No, no. When things settled down and prayers started to be said that was the end of him. Prayer can be all powerful, and that's a fact."

But you don't go to the chapel," Matt blurted out, suddenly realizing he might have said the wrong thing.

"Maybe not too often. I talk to the Man above direct. There's not a day goes by but we have our little chat. I sometimes tell Him where He might be going wrong. Would you credit that?"

"I would," Matt agreed, a little regretful now, not sure how to respond, feeling sorry he said anything. Through his father Matt was well aware that Hal's house was a place where people gathered at night—a rambling house. Stories were exchanged, tea was served, small money games of cards were played. Sometimes poitín was brought along. To change the subject he said, "Did anyone see a ghost lately... Hal?"

"Now that you ask I had a strange experience myself only last week there. Do you want to hear it?"

"Yes."

Hal reached over and ran his fingers through Matt's curly hair. Matt didn't like this. He drew back. *For God's sake don't let any man touch you,* his mother had pleaded.

"You're young Mattie, aren't you?"

"Matt."

"Ah yes, that's right. I get a bit confused sometimes. A fine cut of a lad. The dead spit of your father."

"What happened?" Matt reminded him.

"What happened? Oh yeh—myself and Dan McEvoy

16

were cycling all the way back from New Ross, well after midnight. We were after visiting a very sick friend of ours." He took off his cap and bowed his head. "We'll hardly ever see that poor man alive again. God be good to him." He put the cap back on. "Anyway, do you know the forge road?"

"Yes."

"We were cycling along that level stretch of road, chatting. It was a bright moonlight night. And do you know what happened next?"

"What?"

"A hare suddenly appeared."

"A hare?"

"Jogging along between the two bikes and we only about four feet apart. There he was. I couldn't believe my eyes. Neither of us could. The hair stood up on the nape of my neck, I'll tell you that much for nothing. McEvoy and myself were kind of paralysed. We pedalled faster but it kept pace with us for about half a mile and then"— he held out his hands—"it just vanished. Into thin air! We got off the bikes and fell in against the ditch. That happened as sure as I'm standing here on this ground. You can ask Dan McEvoy if you don't believe me."

"I do."

"It wasn't a real hare, of course. Oh no, not at all. It was some manifestation from the other side. Hares are mysterious creatures, you can bet your life on that."

"I suppose."

"You can be certain sure of it. Tell me this," he suddenly inquired, "how are things at home?"

"Fine," Matt replied, ill at ease now, wondering what he meant by that.

"How's your wee brother?"

17

"Andy?"

"Yes, Andy. Is he... is he... you know?"

"He's all right."

"That's good, that's good. I'm glad to hear that now. God, you never can tell what you'll come up against. It's a strange old world, no two ways about it. But then, it's not the world but the people."

Matt appeared a bit perplexed. He decided to change the topic again. "Your dog's name is Billy."

"That's right, Billy. Billy the Kid—the fastest gun in the west."

"Mine is called Jimmy. That's short for James. I call him King James, sometimes. Your dog is Billy, short for William. William of Orange, or King Billy, as he's called. And that's the River Boyne," pointing to the trickle of a stream.

"The River Boyne," Hal repeated, taking off his cap and scratching his head.

"Your dog is King Billy and mine is King James. Will we fight the Battle of the Boyne all over again, with the two dogs there?"

"Let the two of them at it? Is that what you're saying?"

"Yes."

"How did you get that idea in your head? The Battle of the Boyne!" He smiled. "Be God you have a fertile imagination, I'll say that for you. Them two won't need much coaxing. So my fella is King Billy? I never though of elevating him to that lofty, exalted station."

"They'd hardly injure each other, would they?"

"They're evenly matched. They have good coats of fur for protection. So the Jacobites and the Williamites march again?"

Hal untied Billy, and both held their salivating dogs,

facing each other. Matt hissed *sssh* through his teeth, and at this command the two half-bred collies, in blind rage, tore into action. A ferocious battle ensued, with the two protagonists tumbling all over the place—in and out of the 'Boyne' a few times, rolling over and over, with dust from the dry clay billowing like smoke. Matt looked on in trepidation. First one got on top, then the other. After about five minutes it became apparent that King Billy was going to carry the day. He was spread-eagled on top of King James, holding him down by the throat.

"Quick, we'll stop 'em! Matt urgently interceded.

"They're all right, don't worry." Hal grabbed King Billy by the back of the neck and, with some difficulty, after first having to tap him on the nose a few times got him to release his grip. Matt pulled King James away.

"Looks like King Billy won again," Matt sadly acknowledged.

"It was a good scrap though. There's good stuff in them two."

The two dogs were panting heavily, still bristling, mad eager for another go. No serious injuries of any sort had been inflicted. Surprisingly, King Billy was the one with a slight trace of blood on his lower lip. The two were held apart. Hal looked down at Matt's forlorn face.

"My fella is a bit too big for yours. Look, he's about an inch taller and his chest is broader. Have a good look at them now. It's like boxing: you don't put a middleweight into the ring with a heavyweight, sure you don't?"

"I suppose," Matt balefully agreed.

"There was nothing much in it now, to be fair to them."

"Not until near the end. I'd better head home. She'll have the dinner ready." In the countryside, the midday meal was the main meal of the day.

"Listen," Hal said, "tell your father now I was sorry to hear—" he tailed off.

"Hear what?"

"Nothing, nothing. Tell him I'll call down one of those nights. We'll go for a couple of drinks—if he's up to it. It might take him out of himself—take his mind off things."

"I'll tell him. So-long."

"Good-luck boy, good-luck."

"Come on," Matt said, and he pulled Jimmy behind him, waiting until they were a safe distance down the lane before setting him loose. He'd lied when he said things were fine at home. He was worried before but he was even more anxious now. He tried to put things out of his mind—to live in the fantasy world he created. What was going on? Why didn't they tell him things? Why was it always *run out and play, we want to talk.*? And what was the matter with young Andy? Why was he sniggering and crying and hiding himself away? Was he the cause of all this—the little runt? And worst of all, why was his father reaching for the shotgun and his mother screaming and tearing it from his grasp? And why was the sergeant of the guards calling? All this trouble. He hated trouble.

Hal was now approaching his abode also. He smiled, saying out aloud to no-one but himself, "The Battle of the Boyne!" He took out and lit a cigarette. "How did he think of it? 'Tis a strange world surely. Oh come on home King Billy till I crown you."

A rabbit suddenly emerged. Straining every fibre of its being Jimmy took off in hot pursuit. The rabbit easily outpaced him, darting into its burrow at the foot of the fence. Jimmys' momentum caused him to crash into the bushes and briars. He gave a yelp as the thorns stung his nose. He sat back on his haunches, ears cocked, looking left and right, as if half expecting the rabbit to re-emerge and commit harakiri.

"What will she have for dinner?" Matt mused. "Today is Friday so it'll probably be fish—maybe caulcannon and parsley sauce—or cream and new potatoes." He gave Jimmy a playful kick on the behind. "King James, you're bloody useless." He picked up a piece of straight stick, held it aloft, then pointed straight ahead and shouted, "Charge!" Boy and dog ran towards the farmhouse.

Homecoming

Helen lives alone on a small farm, a few miles from Dungarvan. It is a picturesque area with truly magnificent scenery. Helen, however, is well aware that no matter how much you might admire and appreciate it, you can't make a living out of scenery. And scenery, in abundance, is here in this beautiful area. The farm, in an elevated location, is mostly surrounded by woodland with colourful rhododendrons now vividly flowering out. A small trout stream flowing into a lake, borders the south side of the holding. To the east, the awesome , majestic Comeragh Mountains tower over the whole plateau of central Waterford. The coastline and Clonea Strand are prominent in the distance.

Dungarvan, a busy, bustling town is expanding rapidly, as are similar sized towns all over the country. European Union money, in large quantities, has been pumped into the economy. The good times, however, are well and truly over. The Celtic Tiger is gone for ever—replaced, people say, by a toothless pussy cat. A recession has the country in its grip. Like old Charlie said some years back, 'we'll all have to tighten our belts.' Helen doesn't understand much about recessions and such matters. Whatever money had been generated through the boom period she didn't appear to benefit much from it. Nor does she really care. Helen is an individual who never harboured any ambition about making money. Her farm is small—thirty four acres. Of this, she rents out twenty one acres to a wealthy neighbouring farmer who, to his credit, treats her fairly. Perhaps he has designs on buying the whole place some day. The stream alone would be very attractive to whatever future plans he might envisage. On the remaining thirteen acres Helen keeps her eleven cows and calves. Free range hens are happy and busy, scratching around the yard, haggard and small orchard. There is a large garden to the rear of the house, producing a myriad of vegetables. Helen loves this garden. In fact, it could be classified as her hobby. The household, for its sole occupant, is practically self-sufficient.

Helen is the eldest of a family of three girls. Her two younger sisters emigrated. Betty, married, is living in Chicago. Jane, also married, is now settled in Toronto. To Helen, who was never outside the country, Chicago and Toronto are magical, far-off places. Being the eldest, she was more-or-less expected to stay at home, to look after her parents when they got old, and to inherit the land. Unfortunately her mother, a reasonably young woman, died suddenly from heart failure. This event, naturally, had a devastating effect on the family. To compound matters further, her father, an extremely heavy smoker, contracted cancer shortly after. He never got over the unbearable, tragic loss, of the woman who meant everything to him. Her father fought bravely and Helen spent all her time looking after him. It was an extremely difficult period as he required constant care. As well as this upheaval in her life, Helen had to adapt quickly to running the financial side of things. It was during this period that she decided to rent out most of the land. Her father finally passed away peacefully.

When her father was active and able she enjoyed

working with him. He was a pleasant man and they got on well together. *That cancer is an awful cross to have to bear down on anyone,* she silently contemplates. Invalided and all as he was, when he died she missed him hugely. Tears often flowed as various memories flooded back. The times they spent together, out in all kinds of weather. The winters could be very harsh on this high ground. The cold and frost tended to linger. Those particularly cold periods, when the east wind whipped across from the snow-capped Comeraghs. The loneliness was now also beginning to get to Helen. She's heard all the scary stories about break-ins in isolated farmhouses. As extra security she decides she'll have to buy some more strong locks. Ireland has become more opulent, but far less safe. It appears all the old values are being cast aside, gone with the four winds.

Helen now decides she'll have a last look at the animals before retiring indoors for the night. She is very much attached to all the livestock on the place. She has a pet-name for each of the eleven cows and looks after the lot extremely well. Satisfied that everything is in order she pauses, studying the yard, the shed, the few small out-houses and the dwelling itself. She sighs a little as she looks about, resigning herself to the fact that a lot of improvements could be done to the place. *If only I had the money!* Her faithful dog Glen is sitting at her feet, looking up into her face. She pats his head a few times. She decides that tomorrow she'll give the yard a thorough cleaning. She recalls when she was performing this task back in early April. In fact, the memory remains vividly etched in her mind...

Betty had written to say that herself, her husband Dave and her two young daughters were coming to Ireland on vacation. Dave had always wanted to visit

Ireland, and they had booked into an hotel in Killarney. The letter stated that they'd be arriving in Shannon on Saturday the fifteenth, and that they intended calling to the farm the following Tuesday. Betty had also telephoned to confirm this. Helen remembers being very excited—but also in a slight panic—over the news. In all the years, Betty had been home only once, briefly, for the funeral. Dave couldn't travel at that time as he was away on business in South Africa. Now she was finally visiting, with her husband and two little girls, Jenny and Rose. Helen remembers how nervous and apprehensive she was as the visiting time approached. She wondered what Dave and the girls would think of the place. She resolved to spend all day Monday cleaning up the yard.

She was engrossed in this task, pushing a wheelbarrow of farmyard manure across the yard when who should arrive along but her American visitors—a day early. The big car swung in the gateway, and she hadn't a chance to run, to wash and change her clothes. (Big cars and other large vehicles used the yard to turn, as the space in front of the house was too narrow.) Red-faced, sweating and flustered, she greeted everyone, after first wiping her hands on her overall.

"Oh God!" she now says, putting her hands to her face, flinching, again experiencing the embarrassment of that occasion.

It all came back to her: straight away Dave had struck her as being a very nice individual. He stood there smiling, a happy, boyish looking, tanned American. He gave her a kiss on the cheek and a hug. Betty hugged her close as well. Betty looked great, laden down with jewellery, as slim and attractive as ever. The years had been kind to her. Betty was the youngest of the three girls, always the prettiest and most popular member of the family. Without it being in any way intentional, Betty, for some reason, always made Helen feel inadequate. They had hired out a car and decided to tour the country a day early. Betty said she had phoned a few times but there was no reply. Helen silently remembers cursing her stupidity for not giving her mobile number.

Then Jenny and Rose: Helen was acutely aware that the two young girls, glancing down at her not-too-clean Wellington boots, were unimpressed either by herself or the appearance of the place.

They had looked at her with a sullen expression, refusing any body contact. In fact, they cowed away from her as if she were some kind of ogre. After blurting an apology for the state she was in, Helen couldn't wait to get inside, to quickly wash, change her clothes and tidy herself.

The bathroom door was ajar, and she remembers hearing Rose say, "She's gross."

Jenny said, "The whole place is gross."

Their parents reprimanded them crossly. Betty said, "For God's sake, behave yourselves! I told you what to expect on a farm."

"That's right," Dave concurred, "and be careful what you say. Remember that's Mum's sister you're talking to."

"She's different," Rose said.

Jenny piped up, "Mum, sure we're not going to eat here? I'll get sick."

"Oh God, what are we going to do with them?" Betty said in despair.

Then when Helen returned to the kitchen, Dave said, "Helen, we're sorry for crashing in on you like this. Now you mustn't put yourself to any bother over us. I'll tell you what we'll do: we'll go in to that little town—Dungarvan, isn't it?—and have a nice lunch in the hotel."

Helen remembers explaining that if she knew they were calling that day she'd have had a meal ready.

"At least now you won't have the bother," Dave said.

The meal in the hotel was fine and nicely served, but Helen didn't really enjoy it. She recollects the way she felt shabby, in her dated green dress, aware of the contrast with Betty's stylish, fashionable ensemble. She was also conscious of her rough, large, work-lined hands. The two girls hardly ever took their gaze off her, watching every morsel she put into her mouth, masticated and swallowed.

After lunch they strolled around the town before returning to the farm. Dave commented on how beautiful the scenery was, how it was true about everyplace being so green. How he couldn't wait to travel around this beautiful country. How Killarney was truly out of this world. He was happy snapping away with his new, top-of-the-range digital camera. He explained the workings of this new technology to Helen. The two girls fell in love with the calves. The calves were tame and allowed themselves to be petted. Glen was suspicious at first, but then seemed to enjoy the attention he was paid. He followed Dave, Rose and Jenny, when they went off through the fields to view the little stream and the lake. Dave brought his binoculars, saying they might spot some wildlife in or about the lake. He said he loved nature in all its habitats.

Helen recalls how she was glad to be finally alone with Betty...

Concerned, Betty said she thought Helen looked tired and drawn. She suggested that maybe Helen was working too hard. "Take things easy," she had said. "What's the use in wearing yourself out, getting old before your time? And listen, you'll have to come over to us now, for a good long break. You're entitled to that much. You have no excuses this time. Hire someone to look after things here." Betty had asked her before, but understood that she couldn't travel on account of their father's ill health.

Helen said she would go over, but in truth she couldn't see herself travelling to Chicago. She imagined herself being awkward and ill-equipped for that type of adventure. She had no experience of big cities, apart from what she saw on television. All this flooded back into Helen's mind. The way Betty quizzed her about people they knew years ago. *How was so-and-so getting on? Did she ever marry?* The questions kept flying. And then the turn the conversation took: Betty asking her straight out had she any romantic attachment. *Did she have a man in her life?*

"A boyfriend?" she had replied.

"Yes, a boyfriend."

"I had one."

"Only the one." Betty sounded surprised. "When you say you *had* one, you're talking in the past tense. So what happened?" she persisted.

"It ended." Helen didn't want to pursue the topic. "It just ended."

"Was it because of the way you were tied up here? You could go nowhere? Was that it? He just got fed up?"

"No, that wasn't it."

"It probably was... I'd say it was." The way Betty had studied her face. The way she continued with a somewhat guilty tone to her voice. "Maybe we should have sent on money? Or worked out some arrangement. Done something. Now I feel—"

"There's nothing you could have done, honestly,"

Helen had reassured her.

When she had said, 'It just ended,' she may have sounded bland or blasé. It was anything but. In fact, at that time her world collapsed beneath her. Jamie was the one bright spark in life that offered her hope. Then all the lonely nights after it ended, crying herself to sleep. Over time she had, more-or-less, come to terms with the inevitable.

"Did you like this fellow?"

"I suppose I did, he was nice," she remembers saying.

"And now you have no-one?"

"I think I'm gone past it at this stage."

"Don't say that! I hate that defeatist expression."

"Anyway," Helen had added, "I'll let you know if someone turns up. Miracles never cease. But you met a really nice person in Dave. He's very pleasant."

"He's a kind person, and a good provider. I was lucky. You know, life is funny," Betty had continued, "When Mam died so young I felt angry with the whole world. I couldn't get to grips with anything. That's why I went to America—to get lost, to try and get away from it all. To be on my own. Then, the way things worked out, if I hadn't gone to the States I wouldn't have met Dave. Who knows what twists and turns life would have taken. Or is our destiny preordained for us, I wonder?"

"Dave is very handsome," Helen had commented. "And the two girls are very pretty."

"Very bold at times too. They'd have you fit to be tied. Helen, I'm sorry if they upset you."

"No, they didn't." Betty didn't miss much.

"It's just that they're not in the habit of something a bit on the yucky side—like a farmyard."

"I could tell that."

"Not the way we were brought up, remember?" Betty reminded her. "We had to pull our sleeves up. Nothing was too hot or too heavy for us. Oh, listen—Jane said she intends coming over."

"Did she? That would be a surprise. How is she?"

'Healthwise, she's fine. Her marriage is going through a sticky patch at the moment. Don't worry, it's not the first time. I was in touch with her. I thought she might have been able to make it—to come over with us. We'd all be together then, like old times... A pity the way things turned out, with Mam going so quick and everything. And then the cancer. Not a day goes by but I think back to the old days."

"I know."

"Not a single day," Betty had repeated, eyes downward.

The time had passed rapidly and the visitors were getting ready to depart. Dave and Betty hugged her again. Dave said they had a marvellous time. After being well tutored Jenny and Rose said, "Goodbye Auntie Helen." The way Betty—before she climbed into the car—had thrust three crumpled one-hundred euro notes into her hand. Helen remembers standing at the gate, watching the big car edge up the lane. Hands waved out the window and she waved back. A sudden surge of sadness had washed over her. She wondered when she would see them all again. She also experienced some relief as, by and large, things hadn't gone that bad—apart from the attitude of the children, which stung a little. They had caught her at her worst and she wondered what Dave really thought. Whatever it was, it was a secret he would keep to himself.

When the car had faded from view she acknowledged

to herself what a lucky person Betty was. She had a grand husband and two fine healthy children. She had looked down at the notes in her hand and experienced a tinge of self-pity. She remembers a tear running down her cheek.

She recollects going back inside to change her clothes —the evening's work still lay ahead. She had found it hard to concentrate on her tasks, her mind still preoccupied with what went on before. She wondered how Betty would react if she had to go back to this type of work. Probably all right, she was that type of person. One thing for certain, Betty would never experience that empty pang of loneliness, that all-embracing emptiness. Having finished the chores Helen had gone inside, accompanied by her solitary companion Glen. Another night stretched ahead, just sitting there, half her mind on a magazine, the other half on the television.

She remembers the presents again, standing there on the table: the box of biscuits, the flowers, the large box of Black Magic. She remembers half-filling the vase with water and putting in the flowers.

At Twenty Paces

There are dogs and dogs in it. Some dogs are called names like Spot, Shep, Patch, Brandy, etc. Other dogs are called abbreviations of Christian names, such as Sam, Ben, Jack, Timmy or, as in this narrative—Bobby.

Whatever line of mongrel breed begot Bobby it meant he inherited the long legs of the greyhound in conjunction with the tough upper-body strength of the terrier. It also meant he was a deadly hunting dog, combining the fleetness of the hound with the ruggedness of the terrier. Bobby had the ability to pick off a rabbit in full flight. Not many dogs could out-sprint a rabbit—even the greyhound, over a short distance. On the odd occasions when the rabbit had too far a start the poor creature still didn't make the safety of the briar fence as, invariably, he was shot dead by Bobby's master, Darkie O'Rahilly.

Darkie's real name was Cornelius O'Rahilly, but Cornelius was a somewhat difficult word for people to get their tongues around—and they couldn't very well call him Corny. The main reason he was called Darkie was on account of his jet black hair and sallow complexion. Darkie and Bobby were a lethal combination as far as the rabbit population of Portlaw was concerned.

Darkie had long since given up any form of regular employment. That type of back-breaking work was only suitable for 'fools and horses', as he often joked. He discovered he could make a far better living selling rabbit meat to his appreciative customers around the village. An oven-ready rabbit netted him half-a-crown. He sold, on average, around sixty rabbits a week. It meant he had an income of close to eight pounds, far more than he'd earn working for the farmers—or even that much sought after job in the local tannery.

"They can stick their bloody job," he often said to his friend and accomplice Fat Ned. Edward Dempsey was nicknamed Fat Ned because of his propensity for devouring large quantities of fat meat at the various thrashings around the parish. He was especially partial to fat bacon and cabbage. Fat Ned, whenever he could make the time, accompanied Darkie and Bobby on their hunting excursions.

This suited Darkie fine, as Fat Ned was the one delegated to carry the rabbits. His shambling hulk could be heard panting heavily as he brought up the rear, rabbit carcasses slung over each shoulder. The local housewives were delighted with the arrangement. Rabbit meat was used for stewing, baking, frying, or whatever method was favoured by the cook. The ladies became expert at turning out wholesome cheap dinners. Darkie was on hand to advise them on the various mouth-watering recipes he had picked up on his rounds. A substantial, healthy stew could be served up for the whole family centred round the rabbit, adding in potatoes, carrots, onions and perhaps some other vegetable of choice.

Fat Ned and a couple of other men helped Darkie spend some of his weekly largesse in the local hostelries. When he had a few pints inside him he usually began to laud the praises of Bobby, saying there never was a dog like him in the village of Portlaw.

"That dog is worth his weight in gold. I love that dog." Then he'd add in a slurred voice, "I love that dog a lot more than any of you sons of bitches."

Then someone might laugh and say, "You're some old son of a bitch yourself, Darkie. Anyway, give him another pint."

Fred Crawley, the pub owner would retort, "Sure, maybe he have enough—he won't be able for them hills tomorrow."

Blackie would then look up under his eyes, snorting, "You shut up! You shut your big fat ugly gob, you hear me?" Nobody minded this turn of phrase. This type of banter was par for the course, not to be taken seriously.

Darkie might then put his arm around Fat Ned's shoulder saying, "Poor old Fat Ned here is me best friend," giving him a shake, "aren't you?"

An event occurred at the weekend which was a cause of distraction and disruption to Darkie's routine: Word arrived that his older brother, Billy, had died in Manchester. Darkie hadn't seen him for over ten years but it was decided he'd travel over for the funeral.

Big Mouth Bailey suggested in the pub—in bad taste, it must be said—that Darkie might take in a Manchester United match when he was over there. A hush descended on the place as Big Mouth realized he had put his foot in it again.

Darkie merely commented, "What else can you expect from a pig but a grunt." Relieved, the babble of talk resumed.

Darkie headed off by road, rail and boat for Manchester. It was a long time since he was in England and he wasn't particularly looking forward to the trip. He succeeded in getting there anyhow and teamed up with other members of the family who happened to reside in Britain. Emigration was rampant back in those days. Billy's funeral arrangements were treated with the decorum, solemnity and respect it deserved. He was laid low to the sound of sobbing from his wife Josie and daughters Alice and Lucy. The chief mourners had a meal afterwards in the hotel, followed later still by the men retiring to a nearby pub. They reminisced about Billy for a considerable time, resurrected all the good stories about his adventures in Ireland and England. He was a bit of a ladies man and they laughed over some of the escapades he got involved in. After exhausting the tales about Billy the conversation reverted to Portlaw and its environs. People might emigrate but the old place is always there in their hearts and minds.

Back in Portlaw a big event was taking place—the week long, once-every-three-years mission, was in progress. It was an occasion of faith renewal, well heralded in advance by the local priests. People were warned to be at their best behaviour and to attend the mission without fail morning and evening. The two missioners had duly arrived and taken up residence at the parish priest's house. A little portable shop had been erected outside the church gates selling religious paraphernalia. The tried and trusted agenda was adhered to: one missionary was a calm, pleasant, peaceful individual who espoused the joy of God and the value of prayer. To relieve the pressure in the church and get people to relax, this man sometimes told little jokes. The jokes may not be that humorous but the congregation laughed as if they were the funniest jokes they ever heard in their lives. The second missionary was the complete antithesis of the other. He roared and thundered off the pulpit about sin and damnation, hell-fire and brimstone, proceeding to frighten the living daylights out of the congregation. In the shop on Tuesday morning, after a particularly explosive performance the previous evening, one elderly lady asked another what she thought of the two missioners.

"The small man is a grand fella," the second woman replied, "but the other one is a ferocious man altogether."

Mary Jane and Robert Lacey were a courting couple, who lived about two miles from the Five Cross Roads, five miles from Portlaw. They cycled together, diligently, to the mission each evening. Robert was absolutely known as nothing other than Bobby—the same name as Darkie's dog—ever since he was five years old. He was stone mad about Mary Jane. He could hardly keep his hands off her. All he wanted was to kiss and cuddle her in his arms. They were due to marry in two months time. Mary Jane was a religious girl who believed in no 'monkey business' before marriage. She spent a lot of her time warding off Bobby's advances. She was also very superstitious, as were most people back then. Mary Jane believed in the spirit world and in ghosts generally.

Another event occurred in the village around this time which dictated that secrecy would be of the essence— otherwise a murder would surely tarnish the good name of the village. Bobby, the dog, was left in the care of Fat Ned whilst Darkie was in England. Strict instructions were issued as to how he was to be fed and cared for. None of the other 'whores' ghosts' were to take him off up the woods. Coming towards evening, with the village on the quiet side, Fat Ned decided he'd take Bobby out on a hunt. Darkie lived alone and his abode was a kind of open house where people came and went. Fat Ned spent a lot of his time there. Without permission he took down Darkie's gun and located a few cartridges in a drawer. Dog and man then slipped out of the village in a determined mode.

"Couldn't hit a barn door at twenty paces," Fat Ned muttered. "I'll show 'em."

A mile from home, on high ground, with one rabbit already in the bag, Fat Ned, all tensed up, observed Bobby getting excited, circling a knot of furze. He was determined to use the gun this time. Out flashed a rabbit, off flashed Bobby, up flashed the gun. A shotgun blast punctured the air.

What Fat Ned saw next made his blood run cold and his face turn ashen. He started to shake, whimper and quiver, for there stretched out in front of him, in the last throes of death, lay Bobby. As if bidding this cruel world adieu, one of Bobby's back legs gave a final twitter.

Fat Ned went down on his knees beseeching Bobby— "Get up, get up!" but Lazarus would have stood a better chance. Bobby was as dead as a dodo, riddled with lead-shot, a direct hit.

"Christ above, he'll kill me, he'll kill me," Fat Ned mumbled over and over, sobbing, hitting the ground with his two fists. He eventually quietened down, realizing he had to take decisive action. He thought long and hard. *He disappeared after a fox. That was the last I saw of him. He could be trapped down a fox's den. That sometimes happens, but dogs dig themselves out after a few days.*

He looked around, making sure he was unobserved, picked up Bobby's bloodied remains and carried him to where there was a heavy covering of briars, gorse and furze. In a state of dire panic he flung Bobby into the middle of this thicket. He involuntarily crossed himself. An ignoble ending to a noble hound—to the greatest rabbit hunter the parish had ever seen. Fat Ned then returned to the village and spread the word that Bobby was missing in action.

Back in Manchester, the following night after the funeral, Frank and Darkie had settled in at Frank's local. Frank lived in Manchester and as he had a spare bedroom he accommodated Darkie for the couple of nights he intended staying.

Early in the night, at the pub, they were reverential, looking the part of mourners to their dearly deceased brother Billy, but, as the night wore on they succumbed to the general bonhomie of their surroundings. They found themselves in good company. A sing-song started up.

Eventually, after much persuasion, Frank went over, grabbed the microphone and sang 'Slievenamon'. Darkie took this as a cue to contribute to the proceedings himself. He felt sure this is what Billy would have wanted. What good would moping do? He had a good strong singing voice. His version of 'Dirty Old Town' brought the company to its feet.

The English present wanted to hear some rebel songs. "Come on Darkie"—they had got his name right—"give us a rebel song."

Darkie was a little puzzled by this request, but if the English wanted a rebel song that's what the English would get. With gusto, he belted out 'James Connolly the Irish Rebel', followed by a powerful rendition of 'Boolavogue'. He brought the house down, and when he returned to his seat there were half a dozen fresh pints waiting.

Frank and Darkie had a great time, and stumbled home together at around twelve-thirty, singing in turn a verse or two of 'Whiskey in the Jar'.

The next morning Darkie awoke with a fierce hangover. He put his hands to his brow and mumbled, "How the hell am I going to make Portlaw today?"

Fat Ned had organized a search party of seven men to scour the hill where Bobby 'disappeared.' This was a hill overlooking the ruins of Kilmoganny Church, located about a mile away from the actual hill where the fatal deed occurred.

"He took off in that direction," Fat Ned pointed. "I heard him barking over near that clump of briars. Honest to God, that's the last I saw or heard of the poor old dog. I spent ages looking for him. Look at me, I'm all cut and scratched from briars."

The men spread out, whistled and called "Bobby, Bobby!" over and over. This futile search lasted for nearly two hours, with Fat Ned orchestrating the proceedings. The searchers traversed the hillside in all directions.

"There could be badgers around here too," Fat Ned suggested. "He could be trapped in one of them underground tunnels." Eventually the search was called off and the men, tired, started to walk back towards the village.

"You'll get it in the neck tonight when Darkie gets back," one of the men stated, a comment Fat Ned didn't need reminding of.

The highlight of the mission had arrived. This was it. This was the big one. This was Thursday night—the night of the sixth commandment. The church was packed to the rafters. The congregation sat transfixed with expectancy. In a middle pew sat Bobby Lacey and Mary Jane, their clothes wet from a shower after cycling down. If the congregation were expecting fireworks they got it in droves. The Ferocious Man Altogether was in full flow. He railed off the pulpit about the sins of the flesh. He roared and screamed, jumped up and down, and a woman close to the pulpit said afterwards that she spotted flecks of froth on his lips.

40

Some people of nervous disposition were absolutely petrified. The weather had been close and humid. There was a loud roll of thunder, and a flash of lightning illuminated the missionary, with his arms outstretched, silhouetted against the backdrop of the stained glass window. A well-read man said he looked like a spectre from Dante's Vision of Hell.

"You have two choices," he told the hushed congregation, "Go the way of the Lord and you will hear the loving voice of Jesus calling you to his bosom." Then lowering his voice, added with menace, "Or you can travel the path of evil, where you will hear the voice of Satan," raising the tone again, "calling you to join him in the hobs of hell for all eternity. Yes, the devil's tentacles are there to ensnare your soul, make no mistake about it. So listen tonight, listen to who's voice you want to hear. Is it the loving voice of Jesus calling you, or is it the voice of evil, the voice of Satan you will hear?"

There was another roll of thunder and another flash of lightning. Mary Jane pressed close to Bobby, her body trembling.

If things were a trifle uncomfortable for the congregation in the church they were far worse for Fat Ned. Darkie had him down on the floor, was kneeling over him, pummelling him with his fists.

Fat Ned was yelling, "Stop! Stop!" He was kicking his legs in the air and using his arms and elbows to ward off the blows.

"You son of a bitch," Darkie was hollering, "I left you Bobby for a couple of days while I buried me poor brother and look what happened. I'll feckin' kill you!"

The blows he rained down on Fat Ned were only half-hearted ones, however. He didn't really want to hurt the old devil. His actions were driven out of sheer frustration. He stood up. Fat Ned struggled to his feet also, brushing himself down, none the worse for wear.

"I'm sorry Darkie," he said. "You don't know how I feel. I'm as fond of that dog as you are."

"Like hell you are! No one was to take that dog anywhere. No one!"

"I know, I know."

"I'd give my right hand for that dog. I'd swing for that dog."

"Like I said, he could be trapped in a burrow. He could dig himself out." Pointing, " He might be scratching that door in the morning."

"He'd better be, or you might be a dead man yet."

"Tim Doyle's dog turned up after four days. Listen Darkie, come on across to Crawley's and I'll buy you a drink. It'll do you good, after the journey and all."

"I could do with something right now" Darkie grabbed the ash plant that he carried everywhere and the two of them crossed the road. Crawley's was the only pub in the village where a drink might be available. All the other pubs shut their doors during the mission. Crawley's blacked out the front of the premises but access could be gained to a dimly lit back room if the correct tap was made on the window. Darkie and Fat Ned were duly admitted. Inside were a few lost souls—including Fred Crawley himself—who didn't actually believe in the divine. Commiserations were expressed to Darkie over the loss of his brother and his dog.

"A double blow, a double whammy," Blackie responded.

When Fat Ned went to pay for the two whiskies, Fred Crawley said, "Have this one on me. And my sympathies again, Darkie." They thanked him.

The conversation appeared to centre round the mission. "I hear the tall fella is a terrible man altogether," Big Mouth Bailey commented. "He'd put the fear of God in you, boy."

"He'll give 'em hell tonight," Terry the Beard chuckled. "Tonight's the night about bed-hopping and coveting your neighbour's wife."

"The wives will be giving their ould fellas the cold shoulder tonight, that's for sure," Big Mouth cackled. "Oh be God, it'll be faces to the wall for the next week or so. Oh boys, oh boys!"

Blackie was still in a morose, black mood. He tossed down his whiskey and suddenly grabbed Fat Ned by the collar of the coat.

"Listen, we're going up to that wood right now."

"Not now, not at this hour!" Fat Ned wailed. "Me legs are bet. I'll collapse. Listen to that rain. There's thunder and lightening going."

"You see this plant," Darkie holds out the ash plant in a threatening manner. "If you say 'no' once again I'll break this off your thick skull. I'll call him. He'll know my voice. If he's there at all he'll come to me. Drink that down."

"I'll show you the spot," Fat Ned now said. "But I'm coming back here then. You hear me? You wouldn't put a dog out tonight, sure you wouldn't?" he said, looking around for support. "That lightning is dangerous. It's the hill beside the old Kilmaganny church."

"Shut up and come on."

"Be careful going out," Fred Crawley said. "Don't let anyone see you." Out they went.

"Blackie can make awful threats," Terry the Beard commented.

Old Ted the Philosopher was sitting there, sucking on

his pipe. Old Ted was considered a man of wisdom. He looked up.

"Ah, sure he's all bluster. He didn't kill anyone yet. He's going to miss that dog—his pocket will miss him anyhow."

"Did you know Billy well?" Fred asked.

"Why wouldn't I?" Old Ted replied. Sure he worked above in the estate. He was a great man at felling trees. A great man at directing the way a tree came down. He could put a marker on the ground and knock a tree on top of it." He taps the pipe on his thigh. "A lot of water has gone under the bridge since Billy left Portlaw."

"He had to leave town in a hurry I believe?" Fred remarked.

"He had mickey trouble," Old Ted confirmed. The others giggled.

"Good man, Billy," Terry the Beard guffawed.

"Some woman up the hills," Old Ted continued. "Her husband was an out-and-out maniac, a lunatic completely. He was after Billy with a slash-hook."

The mission for the night had ended. It was dark and sudden bursts of thunder showers were beating down unremittingly. Bobby and Mary Jane sheltered under a tree for the best part of half an hour. When the rain eased they made another break for it. This time they got as far as the ruins of Kimoganny Church when the skies opened up once more. They went and sheltered in the archway of the ruined building, under the overhanging ivy.

"This place is scary," Mary Jane said. "It's supposed to be haunted."

"Ah, it's not," Bobby responded. "Are you cold?" he asked.

"I'm wet and cold," she replied. "Feel my hands."

"Come here and I'll warm you." He put his arms around Mary Jane, drew her to him and kissed her on the lips.

"We must be careful, Bobby," she said, drawing away.

"I love you Mary Jane, more than anything. We'll be married soon so what difference?"

"There's a big difference. We mustn't do anything wrong. I love you too, Bobby. You know that, don't you? I think about you the whole time." They embraced again, long and hard.

"God, Mary Jane, you're so lovely and soft and warm."

"Bobby, stop! Be careful. You heard what the holy priest said—we must avoid all occasions of sin. Thinking about something is as bad as doing it. He said we'd hear the voice of the devil calling—"

She suddenly pulled away from his embrace, cocked her head sideways, listening. "What's that?"

"What's what?"

Then they both heard it—that awful, nerve-jangling sound, booming down from the nearby hill, 'Bobby! Bobby!'

Mary Jane, in a sudden state of near collapse, panicked. "Oh God help us, it's him! It's the devil! Oh Jesus, Mary and Joseph help us." She ran and jumped up on her bicycle. "Oh Jesus, Mary and Joseph assist us!" She started to peddle furiously towards the Five Cross Roads.

Bobby had also grabbed his bicycle. He paused for a couple of seconds, and then heard it again, "Bobby! Bobby, come here."

"Christ Almighty!" He was stronger and had more peddle power than Mary Jane. He soon caught up with, and passed her out.

She wailed after him, "Wait for me! Wait for me!"

The mission finally ended. The people had renounced the devil with all his works and pomps. A certain feeling of anti-climax had descended on the village. The Grand Fella and the Ferocious Man Altogether had gone their merry way—back to the Mission House for a few days rest, to recharge the batteries. Old Ted the Philosopher was sitting on the wooden seat at the end of the street. Jim the postman arrived along on his bike. On spotting Old Ted he crossed over, remained sitting on the bike with one leg on the footpath. They started to chat about the forthcoming general election. Darkie and Fat Ned came round the corner on their two bicycles. Hands waved a greeting. The two continued on up the road heading in the direction of Carrick-on-Suir.

"I told Darkie about this Halligan man outside Carrick who's supposed to have a great breed of terrier pups for sale," Jim the postman remarked. "I'd say that's where they're striking off for."

"Probably," Old Ted agreed. "You know what I'd say about the whole thing."

"No, what?" Jim asked eagerly.

"Don't quote me now, but I wouldn't be one bit surprised if Fat Ned accidentally shot that dog. He was seen with a gun."

Jim the postman struck his fist off the handlebars of his bike for emphasis, "You know something, you could be right! You could have hit the nail straight on the head. Sure everyone knows Fat Ned couldn't hit a barn door at twenty paces."

Smitten

Lily and Poacher are sitting by the fire in the backroom—or what used to be called the snug—of a very old country licensed premises. They are conversing with Bridgie, the proprietress. The accoutrements one associates with this type of business are in evidence: a nice oak table with accompanying oak chairs occupies the centre. There is seating around the sides with another few small tables. Hanging on the walls are enlarged photographs of family members, long since deceased. A few old posters advertising alcoholic drinks also adorn the walls. Like most long established pubs a lot of timberwork is on display.

Poacher is thirty-one years old, strong and wiry, of medium build, wearing Wrangler jeans, an open-neck shirt and a jacket. Lily is twenty-two years old, blonde haired, blue eyed, about five feet seven inches tall, slim and attractive. She is wearing jeans also, a blouse and pink jumper. Bridgie, a tall, dark haired woman is touching the seventy mark. She is wearing a long dress, has beads draped around her neck and bangles on her wrists. She is a pleasant woman, usually with a ready smile. However, she is driven to grumble a lot lately as the licensed trade is somewhat in the doldrums. For the moment, Lily and Poacher are the only customers.

"You know, it all adds up," Bridgie is saying. "Even the coal for that fire costs money. All the overheads have to be taken into consideration. Everything is gone up in the moon. There's no sense to it. No sense at all."

"You're right, Bridgie," Poacher agrees, "things are gone to hell."

"The government, God blast them, are after killing off the pub trade," Bridgie moans. "Look around you, you can see the way things are gone. It's as plain as the nose on your face."

"I'd say you're right," Lily now concurs. "Driving along some nights you'd hardly see a car outside most of the pubs."

"Then they'd try to tell you the smoking ban had no effect," Bridgie adds, placing a couple of logs on the fire. "Be Christ above it had a big effect. People standing outside the door like idiots. The women won't tolerate it anyhow. Late at night they can smoke away here, if they want to. They were doing it for the last hundred years."

"I'm not gone on smoking though," Lily asserts. "Lots of people aren't."

Bridgie pretends not to notice Lily's comment, continuing, "And then this bloody drink-driving thing, down on top of everything else. Did you ever hear of any kind of serious car crash on any of the old by-roads around here? Up around these mountain roads where you'd be only doing thirty miles an hour in any case. I never heard of a crash anyhow. Did you?"

"No, now that you mention it," Poacher responds.

"Not up our road anyhow," Lily confirms. "But then our road is more of a lane. The County Council are the whole time talking about tarring it. Somehow I can't see it happening. It's a case of live cow till you get grass."

"That crowd keep saying they're strapped for cash too." Bridgie takes money out of her own purse. "Anyway,

Poacher, here's the money for that salmon, before I forget it."

"Thanks Bridgie." He gives her back a ten euro note. "We'll have the same again—a pint and a vodka and bitter lemon."

"Right, I'll get you that."

"No hurry."

"A pint and a vodka an' bitter," Bridgie repeats as she goes out to the main bar. There is a serving hatch to the room but in mid-week the orders are mostly taken in from the public bar.

"You're not worried about the guards?" Lily queries, with a smile.

"I don't know when was the last time I saw a uniform around here."

"You'd never know though where they'd pop out of."

Poacher glances behind to make sure Bridgie is out of earshot. "I didn't want to say it to her, but the old booze is the cause of a lot of accidents. You can't get away from it. Two guys I went to school with were killed on the road. The two of them were savages for the drink."

"They'd go wild at home if they thought I was here drinking vodka. They'd fly off the handle completely. My mother in particular."

"They're strict, you keep saying."

"You have no idea. My head will be wrong now after those two vodkas."

"It won't. We'll take our time. Sure we're not in any great hurry?"

"No. You're fond of this place, aren't you?"

"I like to give Bridgie a turn," Poacher replies. "She's a sound person. All belonging to her were decent people. Would you rather if we had gone somewhere else? Some-place for a bite to eat, maybe?"

"No, it doesn't matter. I don't care where we go."

"You're not fussy. I like that."

"We're together, aren't we? That's what matters. I was just thinking today—we're together now practically since you came home from England."

Bridgie returns with the drinks and places them on the large table. "Don't be sitting opposite each other like two strangers," she says. "Why don't you sit over here?" She indicates a longish soft-cushioned seat, positioned close to the fire, which could accommodate three people. They cross over. Bridgie now moves a small table in front of them and places the drinks on it. "Isn't that better?"

"Thanks Bridgie, you're a topper," Poacher says.

"Thanks," Lily says, "that's grand."

"Here's your change—or what's left of it."

"Put it in the box. Eddie and Kate might be along yet."

"I hope so. I like to have some few in."

"You always get a good few, don't you? It's hard to beat tradition," Poacher says.

"Nothing at all like it used be," Bridgie assures him.

"You have the poor mouth, Bridgie." Lily jokes.

"Be God, no. The people from the town used to drive out here in droves. A lot of them still like the old country pub. They like to get away from the spit and polish of the big places in town. The drink-driving killed that trade off—wiped it out. This place was always packed on the weekends. There would be a sing-song above in the main bar. God, it was great. In the middle of the week this room here was used for card playing."

"My father looked forward to it," Poacher says.

"That's right—he was a regular. There would be rows over the cards to beat the band. They'd fight like cats an' dogs. But that was all part of the fun, you see."

"I used hear him on about it—about who played the wrong card."

"If only this room could talk," Bridgie says, her eyes wandering about. "This room has an atmosphere to it. Do you feel it?"

"I suppose," Poacher muses, glancing about also. "Being so old, maybe, gives a certain feel of history to it."

"The timberwork is lovely," Lily adds, "It makes all the difference."

"Many's the match was made here in this room" Bridgie informs them.

"That so?" Poacher says, in a slightly bemused tone.

"Here, in this room?" Lily also expresses her curiosity.

"Yes, here in this very room. It was renowned for it. When I was a very young girl I remember seeing shy, awkward young women, meeting similar types of men. Now some of them men mightn't be that young, mind. Their fathers would be with them and another—a go-between, or matchmaker, if you like. A deal would be struck and money would change hands the same as any fair day. A little celebration would then take place."

"I could imagine," Lily exclaims. "This room could tell stories for sure then."

"They were mostly farming stock," Bridgie continues.

"Most of those arranged marriages turned out all right, didn't they? Poacher queries. "That's what I heard anyhow."

"Oh be God they did," Bridgie assures him. "There was no divorce back then. It was a question of when you enlisted you had to be prepared to march. Sure couples break up nowadays at the drop of a hat."

"It must have been hard on the girls," Lily reflects.

"Some poor girls had little choice," Bridgie explains.

"Times were hard. It was either marriage or the convent for a lot of them. So, as you can see, a lot of important, life-changing events started here in this old room. Hopefully most of the people who met here got on fine afterwards. They probably grew to love each other in their own way and enjoyed life. And enjoyment is what it's all about. Remember the old song, Poacher?" She commences to sing: *Enjoy yourself, it's later than you think.*

Poacher responds: *Enjoy yourself, while you're still in the pink.*

Bridgie continues: *The years go by as quickly as a week.*

Together: *So enjoy yourself, enjoy yourself, it's later than you think.* All three enjoy a little laugh.

"And remember, the words of that song are spot on. I'll leave you to it now. If you want anything just tap on that hatch with a coin." She winks. "You know, it's nice to see the two of you here together in this room. This room, where romance blossomed for so many." Bridgie retires to the main bar area.

"Romance blossomed!" Lily smiles. "I wonder did it? Bridgie likes her bit of fun."

"She always did, for as long as I know her. I'd say it's her manner that draws people in. She's still doing okay. Don't mind what she says. Later on she'll have a good few customers here."

"What she said," Lily ponders. "Hard to imagine people haggling over the worth of a woman. Did they examine her legs I wonder—or her teeth? It sounds awful." She then adds coyly, "How much would you think I'd be worth?"

"Oh, about half a dozen heifers. Maybe a few sheep thrown in to seal the bargain."

"Is that all? I thought I'd be worth a good bit more."

"It would be hard to put a price on you, Lily." He reaches over, and they embrace and kiss for some seconds.

"Will you stay at home for good now?" Lily asks.

"I don't know. I probably will."

"Do they want you to? I hope they do."

"They're shoving on a bit. My father's getting a bit shook now for any kind of heavy work."

"I suppose." There is a slight pause. "Do you like the poaching?" Lily asks.

"In a way. It's a bit of handy money. It's something that gets into you."

"At night, on the river, on your own? It sounds a bit scary and dangerous to me."

"It's the cold that gets you, more than anything. My feet, at times, would feel like two slabs of ice, my fingers might be hanging off me with the frost, and then the wind whipping up the river would cut through you."

"Aren't you foolish so. You must be mad."

"Maybe I am. Mad is probably the right word."

"Anyway, poaching is illegal."

"I know. That's where part of the thrill is."

"Knowing the bailiff is after you?"

"It's all part of it. A kind of cat-and-mouse thing."

"My father says that anything that is illegal is sinful."

Poacher grins. "Sinful! That aspect never entered my head. Your parents are fairly strait-laced alright."

"And religious," Lily volunteers. "The rosary at night lasts about half an hour—prayers for this, that and the other. They hardly go anywhere, only to whatever kind of service might be on in the church. Are you religious?"

"No, not that much," Poacher replies. I only go to please them at home. That's about the size of it."

"But then, you were in England for a good while."

"What do you mean by that?"

"Pagan England. People lose their faith when they go to England."

"A lot of those things you hear are exaggerated."

"Did you like it over there?"

"Fair enough. It was okay, I suppose. Look, it's like this, you meet good and bad everywhere. One thing you learn quick enough and that's how to take care of yourself. I'll tell you one incident that happened to me: one day, for no apparent reason, this big gorilla hit me a haymaker and sent me flying. I got up, feeling a bit dazed, but what he didn't know was that I had a half brick in my fist." He stands up to demonstrate. "We circled around each other, looking for an opening. Suddenly I saw me chance, and I hit him full force on the jaw with the brick, and—"

"You flattened him," Lily interjects.

"Flattened him! You know something, I'd swear to God he didn't wake up yet." He sits back down.

"Did you meet many girls over there?" she queries.

"A few, on and off."

"What were they like? Were they decent?"

"God they were—all of them."

"I hear stories about girls leaving themselves down when they go to England."

"I don't know about that. Some, maybe."

"Did you ever sleep with any girl over there?"

Poacher is a trifle taken aback. "No… no I didn't."

Lily smiles. "You hesitated."

"I didn't."

"Anyway, I shouldn't have asked you that. It's just that I feel I'm a bit of an innocent at large. Nancy and Kate are a lot more streetwise. I notice them laughing behind my back sometimes, over something stupid I said. Maybe it's the way I was kept down so much at home. I've a lot to learn."

"You're fine the way you are, just fine."

"You think so?"

"I'm certain sure of it," he emphasizes.

"I'm glad you think that. Sometimes the others tell jokes that I don't see through. That's when they giggle too."

"Don't mind them. They're older than you anyhow."

"Would you say Eddie and Kate will marry?"

"Probably. They're together long enough anyhow."

"Did you ever think of it yourself?"

"Most single people do, I suppose. Do you?"

"I'd like to be married to someone I really cared about. I'd like to be cuddled up close to him in bed, listening to the rain lashing off the window panes. Feeling secure, comfortable and loved. It would be my dream."

"A cold, wet, stormy winter's night," Poacher adds.

"Just lying back, listening to the gale howling outside. Thinking of the poor old trawler men out at sea, getting tossed around like corks."

Poacher runs his fingers through Lily's hair. "Lily. I like that name. 'Lily of the valley.' You live in a valley an' all."

"What are your folks like?" Lily asks. Are they old-fashioned and strict like mine? But then, you're independent of them. You flew the nest years ago. I should have left too. Gone away someplace foreign. Travel is educational. I'd be the butt of nobody's joke then."

"You're not. Don't take any notice of them other two. You mentioned *years* there. I am a good few years older than you," Poacher reminds her.

"It doesn't matter. I prefer it like that."

"You sure?"

"Yeh."

"You asked me were my parents strict? No, they're easy-going individuals. Like I said, they're shoving on a bit now. They're getting anxious about me remaining single."

Lily raises an eyebrow. "They are?!"

"Definitely. There's a little house down the road a piece where my grandparents—God rest them—lived. The other day my father said, 'No sign of you bringing home a nice young woman. If you find one now don't worry about us. We'll move down to the little house.' We call it 'the little house.'"

"That was very considerate of him," Lily says. "So there's no impediment then to stop you finding some nice young woman."

"No. I'd have to find her first though. That's the problem."

"That's the problem all right," she agrees, eyes down.

"Not everyone would suit me, you know" he continues. "I'd be very particular."

"Oh I'd say that."

"She'd have to be about five foot seven inches tall, with blonde hair, blue eyes, aged twenty-two, with a nice figure and a big friendly smile. It wouldn't matter even if she was a little bit innocent of the world—or said so herself."

"You're making my cheeks turn red now. When you know me better you might think different."

"Lily, I think you're lovely… That's the truth." She puts her two hands up to his face. "What are you staring at?" he asks.

"You have nice features. You know that—Tony" Lily

responds. They embrace and kiss.

"What Bridgie was talking about…" Poacher says.

"Yes?"

"About this room—she said there was something about this room. You know, I think she's right."

"If those walls could talk," she said.

"The sudden way couples were brought together."

"The way their future was decided," Lily adds. "The way girls pledged themselves to men they hardly knew."

"Not like us."

"No."

"Lily, would it be… would it be too sudden if… if?"

"What?"

"If I asked you to marry me?"

"Are you sure?"

"I'll do it the proper way." He goes down on one knee and takes Lily's hands in his. "Lily, I love you. Will you marry me?"

"Yes."

The Mountain Road

The public bar of Bridgie's licensed premises. Bridgie is standing behind the counter talking to two customers, Tadg and Dave. Tadg is thirty one years old, wearing slacks, open necked shirt and sports coat. He is dark haired, thick set, heavy jowled. Dave is twenty eight years old, with light coloured hair, which is now prematurely receding at the front. He is slim, fit looking, wearing jeans, sweat shirt and lumber jacket. Mad Tim is sitting over in a corner by a table, head bent down, felt hat pulled low, growling away to himself, a half consumed pint of Guinness on the table. He has an old gabardine coat pulled around him, concealing some worn work clothes beneath. He is red-eyed, sallow cheeked, unshaven. Horror of horrors, he is smoking a cigarette.

" How is the food going?" Tadg asks Bridgie.

"Not so bad," she replies. I only do light stuff, you know. I make my own apple tarts. Plenty of apples out in the orchard. It's a great way to use them up. Unlike before, the fair sex are inclined to call in now for a cup of tea or coffee. Funny the way a little small thing like that gets out. The girls like the sweet things."

"It's not the only thing they like," Tadg says, taking a swig out of his pint. "I have something I'd give 'em free."

"Better than any apple tart and cream," Dave adds.

"You're terrible, you know that," Bridgie comments.

"God, I'd like a woman this evening," Dave announces, sipping his beer. "Is it the drink or what, Bridgie? Is that what gives a man the urge?"

"Sure the two of you are married," Bridgie points out. "What would you be doing looking for girls?"

"You can't beat a slice from a fresh loaf," Tadg grins.

"That's an awful thing to say," Bridgie admonishes with a wry smile."

"It keeps the cobwebs from settling. You get tired of ploughing the same old furrow," Dave declares.

"You get tired of it is right," Tadg agrees. "I'm tired of Mandy, to tell you the truth. Nag, nag, the whole feckin' time. She'd drive a man out of his fucking mind. If I knew what I was putting myself in for I'd never have walked up that basterin' aisle."

"My woman is the same. Money, money—she's on about money the whole bloody time. She even resents me having a few jars. And you wouldn't mind but she spends a fortune on herself—on clothes, make-up, her hair. Her fuckin' hair is purple wan day and pink the next. And that's about a hundred euro a touch."

"You're awful men, the pair of you," Bridgie says.

Mad Tim seems a trifle agitated. He jumps to his feet and roars, "He's a bastard! A bastard, a bastard!"

"Shut up down there and be quiet," Bridgie shouts.

Tadg and Dave glance sideways at Mad Tim who sits back down and continues his incoherent conversation with himself.

"Is the whore nuts or what?" Tadg asks in a low voice.

Bridgie replies, also in a low voice, making a circular motion with her finger on the side of her head, "He's a little bit gone alright."

"A little bit!" Dave smiles.

"He comes in here twice a week and drinks two pints. He lives in his own world. Ah, he's harmless, don't mind him. There's not much I can do about it. His father and three brothers are my four best customers. Two is the limit I was instructed to give him. He lives just across the field, so he's not a danger on the road or anything." She crosses over to Mad Tim. "I thought I told you not to smoke in here." He has the butt-end stubbed out at this stage. "It's against the law."

"I wasn't smoking," he says.

"Who was then?" Bridgie asks, as she dispenses the smoke by waving her hands.

"The other man."

"What other man?"

"The other fella."

"There was another fella here?"

"Yeh."

Bridgie shrugs her shoulders in a weary manner, saying, as she returns to the bar, "I didn't see any other fella. Did you see any other fella?" she asks Tadg and Dave.

"Be God we did," Tadg grins over at Mad Tim.

Dave points, "He was standing there in the middle of the floor with his big mickey in his hand."

"Will you shut up. God almighty!" Bridgie exclaims with feigned indignation.

"That's right, that's right!" Mad Tim shouts, half rising.

"Bridgie, I'll tell you a little story " Tadg says. "Some years ago, when I was living at home there was a woman near-by who was a nymphomaniac—or something like that. One man wouldn't satisfy her at all—she had to have three or four on tow. Her husband, a small little guy, was pissed off by the whole carry-on. One night, at around three o'clock, she was dropped off from a car with three men inside. The little fella was waiting up for her. He roared, when she came in, 'This must stop! I'm not goin' to be second fiddle around here any more!' She roared back, 'With the instrument you've got you're lucky to be in the band at all!'"

Bridgie turns away, smiling. "Oh God look down on us."

"Is she still around—that woman?" Dave jokes.

"They split up years ago—went across the pond."

"That never happened?" Bridgie queries.

"Be God it did. Quarer things than that happened."

"Strange things do happen I suppose," Bridgie says, giving the counter a wipe. "What you two should do now is take care of your own marriages. Work at it, you hear me? It's the most important thing you have. Be prepared to look at the other person's point of view. There has to be a bit of give an' take," Bridgie advises.

"What if it's all take and no give? That's a horse of a different colour," Tadg declares.

"You can be sure it's a different bloody colour," Dave agrees. "Some women want it every feckin' way. The hand is stretched out the whole time. It would sicken you. Christ, women!"

"You had a bit of a row today I'd say, did you? The two of you? You're off on a bit of a tear now." Bridgie concludes.

"Rows," Tadg repeats, "we have fuckin' rows the whole time."

"Same here," Dave admits. "I don't know. I think this whole marriage thing is a bit of a lark. 'Marriage is an institution, and who'd want to live in an institution.' Didn't somebody say that?"

"I'd like to hear now what the two ladies in question

have to say about you two. There are two sides to every coin. I'm a firm believer in that. Two sides to every story," Bridgie declares.

"We'll forget about 'em," Tadg says. "Feck 'em. Here Bridgie, give us two more of the same like a good woman."

Dave crosses over and puts his hand on Tim's shoulder. "What's your name?" he asks.

"Tim."

"You like the old beer, Tim?"

"Yeah."

Dave shouts across, "Get a pint for Tim as well."

"You will not." Bridgie interrupts. "He has his quota for the day and that's the end of it. Sure his glass is still half full. Maybe you have enough yourselves too. Who's the driver?"

"We have the two cars," Tadg tells her. "And don't worry about us and the drink. You just keep churning it up."

"It's handy to have a car each," Dave says, "in case we picked up a bit of skirt."

"God, can you think of anything else? You're hardly going to find your bit of skirt in here."

The little Nissan Micra is winding its way along the scenic route, the short cut. Madge and Linda are the two occupants of the car. Both are hovering around the thirty age mark. Madge is brown haired whilst Linda is blonde. Madge, serious looking, on the plump side, is wearing slacks, blouse, blue cardigan and short jacket. Linda is wearing a skirt—she likes to show off her shapely legs—and a jacket to match over a blouse and jumper. Both are nice looking without being head turners. Well, Linda maybe could be classified in that category.

"Isn't that lovely," Linda says, referring to the magnificent panoramic scenery on both sides of the road.

Madge, the driver, allows herself a furtive glance at this magical vista spreading out into the distance. The trees and foliage exude a myriad of colour: light green, dark green, brown, purple, red and yellow.

"If I were a landscape artist I'd make it my business to come up here and paint that," Linda continues.

"Ever think of taking it up?"

"No. I'd probably be no use anyhow."

"You never know till you try. I tried it once but I'm afraid I haven't much talent."

"It would be a grand hobby to have all right."

"You wouldn't want to go off the road up here," Madge says after a pause.

"You sure wouldn't."

"I'm still nervous driving," Madge continues. "It takes a long time to get over an accident. Pictures keep flashing back into your mind."

"I imagine so. It can all happen so quick. And then it could be all over. I mean, your whole life gone—wiped out. Or left paralysed maybe—in a flippin' wheelchair. You're all right now though, aren't you?"

"My back still aches at times. The frosty weather seems to make it worse."

"The girl in the other car..." Linda tails off.

"Yeh, she died—lasted a week, the poor thing. It was all a nightmare... A nightmare."

"And the other man, the driver, was drunk?"

"Drunk as a skunk," Madge confirms. "Anyhow I hate thinking about it."

"I know."

A period of silence descends as they motor along.

They are casually at ease with each other and the silences are comfortable. Linda starts to sing in a low voice, in an absent-minded manner:

> I used to love her, I used to love her once,
> A long, long time ago,
> But it's all over now.
> I have fallen for another—she can make her own
>   way home,
> And if she even asked me now I'd let her go alone.
> I used to see her up the chapel when she went to
>   Sunday Mass,
> And when she went to receive I'd kneel down there
> And watch her pass.
> The glory of her ass.

Linda has a nice soft singing voice and Madge enjoys listening. Other people in a similar situation could grate on the nerves, but not Linda. She sometimes thought that if she were a lesbian she'd probably fall for Linda.

"The glory of her ass," Linda repeats, having stopped her singing, looking sideways at Madge. "A strange line for a song?"

"I suppose it's the context of the song," Madge says.

"I suppose." Another pause.

Fall for Linda! Strange thoughts to be sure, Madge admitted to herself. But somebody once told her that there are lesbian tendencies in lots of women. Didn't girls fall for the pretty nuns at school? A peculiarity, if one could call it so, that was confirmed to her by several.

"The Saw Doctors are from my neck of the woods," Linda states. "Did I tell you that?"

"Yeah, you told me."

"Why do I keep repeating myself? My head must be going."

"Do you like 'em?" Madge asks.

"They're okay. They're on the road a good while now."

"Like The Rolling Stones."

"Or Cliff Richard."

"I like Cliff Richard," Madge says. "Would you say he's gay?"

"I don't know. Just because a person chose to remain single doesn't mean he or she has to be gay. You'd have a fair lot in this country if that was the case."

"Lesbianism is not taken as seriously as homosexuality, sure it's not?" Madge suggests.

"What put that idea into your head?"

"The thought just struck me. I was watching a film on the telly the other night—it was about a relationship between two women."

"Did you like it? Was it enjoyable?"

"It was thought provoking. You know—'different strokes for different folks'. 'It takes all kinds'. You know, that kind of thing."

Linda smiles. "Would Bert be worried if he heard you were discussing lesbianism?"

"Oh God," Madge says, "he'd be a real macho."

"I imagine. I'd say nearly all the Garda would."

They know each other so well that they feel relaxed and at liberty to discuss their thoughts on any given subject. Linda starts to hum that tune again in a vacant abstract fashion.

Madge feels annoyed with herself. Why did she seek to be in Linda's company so much? Linda now yawns, stretching her arms, causing her skirt to rise a little, revealing more of her upper legs. Glancing down, Madge suddenly felt she'd love to run her hand up those lovely white thighs. What would happen then? Probably signal the end of a nice friendship. Still, Linda puzzled her somewhat. She's very attractive, but she never saw her with a man. Am I going cracked thinking things like this! She's right. What would Bert say? God! Coming out of her reverie she suddenly sits bolt upright.

"What's wrong?" Linda asks.

"Nothing."

"Be careful anyhow. Don't doze off."

"Look at this," Madge says, as she rounds a bend coming on a tractor and trailer travelling in the same direction. "I won't be able to pass this fellow unless he pulls over."

Willie Kelly, the tractor operator is in dreamland. He is a worried man, thinking about the fodder situation on his farm—*what if the weather broke in a bad way? Christ above, it's nearly always raining anyhow. The situation's tight, so maybe I'd better buy that dear hay after all. The weather men are warning that this climate change thing is going to bring even more rain.*

He vaguely thinks he hears a car horn over the noise of the tractor, but he's not sure. His side mirror is broken, so he cranes his head to try and catch a back view. He snaps on his left indicator and pulls in at the wide entrance to a forestry plantation. As she passes, Madge flashes her warning lights acknowledging his swift course of action.

"He wasn't the worst," she says. "I was often stuck behind a tractor for miles."

"We're getting close. Will we call to that pub for a cup of coffee?"

"We might as well. Her apple tart is lovely."

Linda glances at her watch. "We're making good time."

"We are. I'm not meeting Bert for two hours yet.

Maybe we'll spend some time in that new shopping centre in Cahir?"

"That's an idea."

Back at the pub, Tadg decides a song might be in order. Holding his head back and closing his eyes like Christy Moore he belts out his rendition of *The Red Rose Café*. Tadg has that distinctive Irish nasal singing voice that Spike Milligan said was 'known and hated all over the world.' Putting his arm round Tadg's shoulder, Dave has joined him for the final verse:

> *Down at the red rose café in the harbour,*
> *There by the port just outside Amsterdam,*
> *Everyone shares in the songs and the laughter.*
> *Everyone there is so happy to be there.*

Madge and Linda come in the door. Tadg and Dave sing the last line again: *Everyone there is so happy to be there.*

"Hallo girls," Tadg says, all smiles.

Madge responds with a curt "Hallo."

Linda says nothing.

"Will you have a drink? Come on over and join us."

"No thanks." Madge replies. They cross over and sit by a table with their backs to Tadg and Dave. Tadg ambles back to Dave.

Bridgie goes to serve the two girls. "What'll it be, ladies?" she asks. "Maybe the same as the last time you were in?" she suggests.

"That'll be grand," Madge says.

"Have you more of that tart and cream?" Linda asks.

"No shortage. Coffee, isn't it?"

"Yes, please."

"Won't be a minute." Bridgie goes off to prepare the apple tart and cream.

The girls have become aware of Mad Tim, who still

has his head down and is mumbling away, raising and lowering the tempo. They wonder should they have bothered calling in here at all.

"Well, what do you think?" Tadg murmurs to Dave.

"I don't know. I'd say they're a pair of snooty bitches."

"Will we give 'em a try?"

"Might as well," Dave answers. "I'm going for the blondie one."

"Why are you always leaving me the ugly one?"

"She's not ugly. All right, take your pick. I don't care."

"No, it's okay, it's okay. I like 'em with a bit of flesh on 'em."

Dave downs a good gulp of Heineken and waltzes across to the two girls, singing en-route:

> *Four and twenty virgins*
> *Went down to Inverness,*
> *But when the ball was over*
> *there were four and twenty less.*

He holds out his hand, "My name is Dave." The offer of his hand is not accepted. "And that fellow back there is Tadg." Tadg gives a little smiling wave. "Will you join us for an old drink?"

"No thanks," Linda says, with a measure of irritation.

Bridgie arrives with the order on a tray.

"Why not?" Dave persists.

"Will you please leave us alone," Madge says with an authoritative voice.

"Can't you see where you're not wanted?" Bridgie interjects, as she places the plates and cups on the table.

"I'll pay for that," Dave offers.

"You will not," Linda says. "Here you are," she passes a ten euro note to Bridgie, "Will that cover it?"

"That's fine, thanks." Bridgie indicates to Dave to

return to his place at the counter. He slowly moves back to rejoin Tadg.

Mad Tim suddenly falls to his knees in front of Madge and Linda. Wild-eyed he looks up, arms outstretched.

"I saw them, the three of them" he shouts. "Jesus Christ, Mary and Saint Joseph!"

Madge and Linda almost fall off their chairs.

Bridgie quickly intercedes. "It's all right, it's all right! Take no notice of him, he's harmless. Come on over here," she says to Tim. She takes up his drink and escorts him to a table at the farthest corner of the room, near the entrance door.

Grinning, Tadg nudges Dave.

"He's a mad hatter. Jesus, me heart!" Linda says.

"We won't linger too long here," Madge advises in a low voice.

"Feck 'em! Linda replies, "we won't let them two bums run us out of the place."

Bridgie returns to the table. "God, I'm sorry about that," she apologises. He startled you, didn't he?"

"Yes, a bit. It's all right."

"Don't worry about it," Linda reassures her. "I see a lot worse than that every day of the week."

"Is everything okay, then?"

"We're grand."

"Good. Thanks."

"They're two dead ducks," Dave says. "We won't get anywhere with them two sticks."

Tadg now ambles across to the two girls. "What's wrong with you anyhow," he asks. "We're only trying to be friendly. Team up with us for the night. Nobody will be any the wiser. We know our stuff. We'll take ye to the heights."

Bridgie intervenes, as Dave joins Tadg, "Can't you see you're interfering where you're not wanted. You have enough drink in you now. You're not fit to drive. I'll phone Cahir for a taxi."

"What are you saying?" Dave responds in a threatening manner. "Fuck you! We'll drive home the quiet mountain road. The fuckin' cops don't even know that road exists."

Tadg is well aware that Dave is an impulsive individual, easily roused. "Come on over and we'll finish our drink," he says.

They were in trouble with the law twice before. Tadg is a little concerned the way things are developing now. They return to their position by the bar.

"Calm down " Tadg says. "We want no more trouble, you hear me? We'll head back to Cahir. We'll give Lacey a shout."

"Right, right," Dave says, looking behind, exclaiming in a loud tone, "They're only two stuck-up bitches, anyhow."

"Go on home with you now," Bridgie says, "and mind your language."

"We will, we will," Tadg replies.

Dave turns on Bridgie again, "Nag nag nag, you're like all the other bloody women."

Bridgie puts her hand on his shoulder as a gesture urging him to go.

"Hold on now, Bridgie. Take it easy. Don't try the bum's rush on us." He holds up a finger. "Our two whiskies! We must drink our whiskey."

"Oh yeh, the whiskey," Tadg repeats. "We'll be off then."

They pick up the two half whiskies. Tilting back their

heads they gulp down the whiskey like two frogs swallowing two flies. They move towards the exit door. Dave bends down and whispers something to Mad Tim.

"Take it easy now on the road," Bridgie warns. "For God's sake go easy. You should have let me get you a taxi."

"Don't worry," Tadg says. "Good-luck."

Bridgie locks the door. She walks back to Madge and Linda, looking relieved.

"I'm glad to see the backs of them."

Madge goes to the window and looks out, as the two cars are heard to start up and drive away.

"That narrow lane, is that the 'quiet mountain road'?" she inquires. Bridgie replies, "Yes."

"Team up with us," Linda repeats. "If they were the last two men left on the planet I wouldn't team up with them."

"Maybe you served them a little too much alcohol," Madge suggests to Bridgie.

"Maybe I did. But they had a lot in them when they arrived. It's hard to know. Running this type of business is not easy."

"I'll put a stop to their gallop," Madge declares, taking out a mobile phone and dialling a number.

"Hello Bert… I'm fine… Listen, you're patrolling the Cahir area, aren't you? Where are you now? Outside the town. Do you know Bridgid McCarthy's public house, at the foot of the mountain? That's it. There's a small, quiet, mountain road leading into Cahir… You know it well. Good… Listen, there are two drunken fellows on that road right now. They were here in the pub… Are they over the limit?" She glances at Linda and Bridgie. "They're about three times over it… One is driving a silver Mondeo and the other a green Corolla… They're not too pleasant, so be careful… Four of you… We just pulled in for a cup of coffee… Linda… A bit, yeh. See you later then. Bye."

She returns the mobile to her handbag.

"They won't bother anyone else for the rest of the day. I'd like to see their faces when they're frogmarched into the station."

"Listen," Bridgie pleads, "don't tell anyone about me selling them too much booze? None of the guards, anyhow?"

"We won't, but you should watch it," Madge replies. "I was implicated in a fatal accident and I don't want to see it happening to anyone again. Those two gone out could well be the cause of one—nothing surer."

"Have another cup of coffee," Bridgie offers, "on me."

"No thanks," Linda says.

"You will, you will," Bridgie insists, hurrying off to prepare it.

Linda shrugs her shoulders. After a little while Mad Tim moves over and stands in front of Madge and Linda. He gestures wildly with his hands.

"Did you see him? Did you see him?" he gasps.

"See who?" Linda asks.

Linda and Madge are more relaxed now, having come to terms with the situation. Also comforted by the fact that the other two are gone.

"The man! The man standing there…"

Bridgie arrives back with the tray.

"Where?" Linda asks Tim.

"Standing there with his—"

Bridgie sternly cuts him short, "What's he saying?"

Tim is afraid of Bridgie and he goes silent. She places the tray on the table.

"Come on now," she says to Tim. "Time to be going

home now. They'll be wondering about you." She escorts him to the door. "Finish up that."

He finishes the remainder of his pint glass.

"That's the good man." As he goes out: "and mind yourself crossing home."

"The others put him up to say something," Madge says to Linda.

Bridgie returns to the table. "Christ above, you never know what to expect next. I'm living on my nerves."

The Ranch

Linda accompanied Madge down to Cahir with the express purpose of borrowing Madge's car and driving out a few miles on the Clonmel road to visit her cousin who she hadn't seen for ages. She remembered, as a teenager, spending holidays at this particular cousin's family farm. She remembered learning how to do the farm chores. All the laughs they had as the 'townie' tripped herself up on numerous occasions. However, she wasn't too long catching up. To travel out there now would be an ideal way of spending a few pleasant hours. They had a lot of catching up to do. But no—it being Madge's birthday, Bert and Madge had both insisted that she join them for dinner at this exclusive restaurant called The Ranch. Linda felt she had no alternative. If her refusal was too adamant they might feel insulted.

The Ranch, a small hotel-cum-restaurant, was approached by a long winding driveway. As they drove up this tree-lined entrance, with the timber fencing on both sides, Linda admired the thoroughbred horses grazing on the lush pastures.

"Larry had a few winners recently," Bert said, straight away conveying that he was on friendly, first-name terms with Larry, the obvious owner of the property.

So far, it all looked impressive, Linda thought, heightening her expectation of what lay in store. Still, wouldn't the two of them be better off coming here on their own, she reasoned. After all, they were engaged. She herself was well aware of the expression *two's company, three's a crowd*. Could it be that Madge was so fond of her precious new car that she was fearful of anyone else driving it? Unlikely—didn't she drive it a few times already? Madge liked her vodka and coke.

Entering the foyer, Linda was struck by the expensive looking paintings, the sunken carpets, the whole opulent old-world charm of the place. After having a look around to saviour the ambience they were directed in to the dining room, with its ornate decorated ceiling, exquisite oak furnishings, and Waterford glass chandelier. A glance at the other diners indicated that they had dressed well for the occasion. Bert was the only one who didn't appear to have bothered.

Now Linda got on well with members of the Garda Síochána. She got to know a good few through her work in the A&E section of the hospital. They often arrived along with victims of domestic violence, or urgent cases where no ambulance was immediately available. Also cases where they interviewed people injured as a result of criminal attack. By and large she found them agreeable and pleasant—they looked well and were good company. Some of her fellow nurses were married to members of the Garda.

But like all large organisations there was always a certain number who would kick against the traces. There was always a small percentage who refused to conform to the standards set by the vast majority. A rogue element, if you like. Linda had already decided that Bert belonged to the latter category. Bert was overweight, with his tummy hanging out over his belt. He hadn't even taken the trouble to shave and was sporting a thick stubble. He hadn't even bothered to change out of his baggy black trousers or his blue shirt. He just added a sports jacket that had by now become too tight for his large frame.

Linda had a certain fixation about cleanliness. Her work required her to deal with some unsightly cases at the A&E. She treated all kinds of wounds and oozing sores— drunks who fell down and were badly injured, liable to spew vomit or strike out whilst being treated. That's why, when she got home from work she liked to soak herself in the bath, or stand under the cascading shower for upwards of twenty minutes. Bert's slovenliness put her off.

Another thing that quickly became apparent about Bert, as they made the trip to The Ranch, was the fact that his feet gave off a particularly foul odour. She wondered what Madge saw in him. How could a woman go to bed with Bert? But then she noticed that Madge too was starting to get careless, of late. She had adopted this particularly irritating habit of poking her finger up her nose, or sticking it in the outer reaches of her ear, taking it out and looking at it to see if there was wax stuck to it. Linda felt sorely tempted to blurt out her distaste a few times.

The waitress arrived along with the menus.

What a knock-down beauty she is, Linda thought to herself. *Why are those Polish girls so pretty?*

The menu looked impressive:

The Ranch three terrines:
foie gras, duck rillette & ham hock
served with apple chutney & blackcurrant reduction
Greenstone Point Riesling

Wild mushroom soup with white truffle oil

Sumaridge Pinotage
Pouilly Fume Domaine Raimbault-Pineau

Cosmopolitan sorbet

Sirloin steak on roasted vegetables with a
braised venison cottage pie
or
Pan-roasted fillet of corbet with crispy potato scales on a confit
of leeks with saffron & shallot sauce

The Ranch opera gateau with a praline mousse

Tea or coffee with petits fours

There was a pianist in the corner of the room playing a nice repertoire of tunes, old and new. His only fault being that he was a little on the loud side. Bert and Madge sat together at the somewhat large table and Linda found it difficult to make conversation. In any case the other two were so engrossed with each other that she was more-or-less ignored. Not that she cared in the slightest—in fact she preferred it this way.

Any clarity of conversation was further hindered by a very loud, monopolizing party who occupied the table directly behind Bert and Madge. She secretly hoped they got a whiff of Bert's feet. She hoped the foul smell seeped across under the table like some form of odious gas. Glancing over she could detect no reaction so far.

The wine waiter arrived and Bert, after studying the list and then looking round for confirmation, opted for a bottle of red house wine. It was usually the cheapest plonk in the place.

Linda leant over and asked Bert how the two drunken motorists behaved earlier on. "Did they create a row?"

"Like I said," Bert answered, "they were awkward and difficult. But we took care of them. We come across them awkward customers on a regular basis. They were well on. They'll get a hefty one. One of them had no insurance, into the bargain."

"They could have killed someone," Madge stated.

"They could have," Bert automatically agreed.

Madge continued with her mantra, "They were as drunk as skunks. They can't say they weren't warned. It's blazoned all over the place—if you drink don't drive. If you live by the sword you'll die by the sword."

All three enjoyed the starter and the soup. Like a large Black Labrador, Bert lapped up the soup with gusto. For the main course Linda ordered the fillet of corbet. Bert and Madge chose the steak. Bert wanted his cooked very rare. The fillet of corbet, when eventually it arrived along was nothing to write home about. Bert's steak was so rare that it looked as if it hadn't been cooked at all.

"Are you staying overnight?" Bert inquired.

"No," Madge emphatically replied.

"Why won't you?" he suggested in hope.

"Tomorrow is a working day. I'd rather go back, honestly."

"In that case," Linda said, "and seeing that it's your birthday, I'll limit myself to one glass of wine. I'll drive home."

"Are you sure?"

"Yes. You can drink away then and enjoy the night."

"Thanks."

"Don't mention it."

Bert looked disappointed that they weren't staying.

He again started to murmur away to Madge. Linda leant back and studied them both across the table. Madge was a primary school teacher. They would eventually marry. The garda and the school teacher was a union that was pretty popular. It meant they would be financially secure for their entire lives. They would probably have, well, maybe four kids—two boys and two girls. The two girls would play camogie and take up Irish dancing. The two boys would play hurling and Gaelic football. All would spend time in the Gaeltacht to further their chances of landing a good job in the civil service.

They in their turn would marry and the whole procedure would carry on and on and on, into infinity.

Linda was also very conscious of the cacophony of loud laughter and remarks from the nearby table. Comments were bandied about such as, "Good luck old boy," A female commented, "He's simply a ghastly fellow!" Then, "Good show," and "You must call over for drinks." Then the sudden overbearing guffaws at some genius's perceived wit.

Bert poured the wine.

Linda put her hand over her glass, saying, "No, thank you."

Earlier Bert had said he did Larry a turn. He looked around now to see if there was any sign of him. The last time he was in here Larry had waived the bill. But on this occasion he appeared to have gone to ground. Bert decided they'd linger on there in the dining room. Larry was bound to emerge from somewhere.

The dessert waiter arrived. Linda didn't eat dessert but she decided to accept it anyhow. It was part of the package and Bert, no doubt, would hardly say no to a second helping. She requested to have her coffee served with the dessert.

Linda took seventy euro out of her purse and passed it to Bert. "That'll cover me—tip and all," Linda said.

"No, no, take that back." Madge handed back the money.

"It's all right, I'll fix that," Bert said, without much enthusiasm.

But Linda was independent. "Do you want me to tear it? That's what will happen." She returned the money.

"That's terrible. You're awful," Madge then said.

The deserts and coffee arrived.

"I don't eat desert." Linda edged her bowl towards the centre. "If you don't mind I'll take this coffee out to the lounge."

As she stood up she announced in a loud tone, "Those loudmouths behind your back are driving me nuts." There was a slight pause in conversation at the table referred to.

Linda moved out to the lounge bar and sank into one of the comfortable armchairs, placing her cup and saucer on a small table nearby. One of the reasons why Linda wanted to sit in the lounge was to observe the two glamorous waitresses traipsing to and fro. One of the two approached her now and politely inquired if there was anything she would like.

"There is," Linda replied. "I'd like you."

The girl smiled, slightly embarrassed, and moved away, saying, "I'm afraid that's impossible."

Linda sighed, thinking how she'd love to have that beauty lying beside her, feeling those blonde tresses against her cheeks, that lovely form entwining hers. Then she thought of Madge again. It was her birthday, so maybe she should get her a drink or something. She'd already given her flowers. She crossed to the bar. Straight away, and for no apparent reason, an animosity seemed to develop between herself and the slight barman, the one with the sallow complexion, the sleek black hair and thin moustache.

"What's the cheapest wine you have on your list?" She asked.

"This one," he pointed, with faintly disguised distain. "This Chilean one is cheap at thirty euro."

"You call that fuckin' cheap?" she blurted out. You'd probably get it at Lidl or Aldi for five euro."

He put his fingers to his lips, "Ssssh, please watch your language."

"I'll watch what I like. Here, I'll take it." She counted out the money using all the small change she could muster to make up the last five euro.

"You're not on the game, I hope."

"What? What are you saying?"

"We have standards around here."

"I don't care what you have. What exactly did you mean by—?"

"Nothing." He walked away.

"Come here a minute…"

But he ignored her, and served two other customers.

She took the bottle of wine in to Madge and Bert, noticing it was the same brand they'd had with the meal. They thanked Linda profusely.

She returned to her seat still thinking of what the barman said. She became aware of three Fancy Dans at the bar giving her looks. Did she appear a bit of a tart or something? Was it the clothes she had on? Eventually one of the three strode over.

"What's a lovely, beautiful girl like you doing, sitting here on your own?" he said. "Do you mind if I join you?"

He was preparing to seat himself when Linda said, "I do."

"Oh," he said, halting in mid-posture, and straightening up again.

"It's like this," she explained. "My husband"—pointing to the dining room—"is a former boxer and he's a very dangerous, jealous guy. You have a nice nose and I'd hate to see it splattered all over your face."

"Oh," he said again. "In that case it was nice meeting you," and he scampered back to his companions. After a short discussion they looked over at her and smiled.

The piano music drifted out to where she sat. The pianist was now playing *Down at the Red Rose Café in the Harbour*. Linda thought again about the two guys in the pub earlier on. When all's said and done they weren't really all that bad, she mused. What were they trying to do? Trying to score—trying to get off the mark. Most men were the same. She was aware that at the time she more-or-less implied that she wouldn't pee on them if they were on fire. But now she felt kind of sorry for them. If Madge wasn't so prudish they could have palmed them off with a few jokes or something. Instead of that she'd stitched them up. They'd surely have made their way safely home by the route they planned. What would happen now? A heavy fine and off the road for two years, more likely. When they lose their cars it could mean losing their jobs as well.

Then what she was told about Madge and the accident: Madge was renowned as a fast driver. The guy in the other car wasn't 'drunk as a skunk,' to quote Madge. He was just marginally over the legal limit. A girl was killed though, and Madge was exonerated. She was also awarded a large sum of insurance money. That accident still worried Madge though, Linda felt.

She decided she'd have another cup of coffee. She crossed over to Sundance with the moustache. He appraised her coldly.

"How much is a cup of coffee?"

"Four fifty."

"Four fifty!" she gasped in disbelief. "You're joking? That's outrageous!"

He shrugged his shoulders in a haughty manner. This one, he felt, was more of a nuisance than anything else. He had his pride. He didn't have to listen to this cow complaining. After all, he was part of The Ranch. He turned to move away.

"I'll have a glass of water."

"Tipperary or Ballygowen?"

"Tap water."

"We don't serve tap water."

At that moment a man with a managerial bearing and a grey pin-stripe suit was passing. Linda clicked her fingers in his direction. He came over.

"Listen," she said, "I just spent nearly a hundred euro in there," pointing to the dining room, "and now this dickhead won't serve me a glass of tap water."

"I'm sorry," he responded. The last thing he wanted was a scene of any sort.

He indicated to the barman to comply with her request, saying, "It's all right, Bruno."

To Linda he then added, "I hope you enjoyed your meal?" expecting her to answer in the affirmative.

"I didn't."

"In that case I'm sorry again." He flashed a false, watery smile and continued on his way. Bruno looked none too pleased.

"You be careful about the type of remarks you pass,"

Linda said, still smarting over what he had said. "You hear me?"

"What remarks? I don't know what you're talking about."

"You know well."

"Here you are. Would you like a slice of lemon in it, Madame?"

"No." He gave her that cynical look again as he moved up the bar.

"Far from 'Madame' you were raised, you little prick," Linda flung after him. He appeared as if he was about to turn and come back but there was an impatient looking customer at the other end of the bar. Linda returned and relaxed back in the comfortable upholstered leather seat. She closed her eyes, savouring the soothing music from next door. She wondered why she was so impulsive on occasions.

Maybe she should have said nothing to that guy behind the bar. After all he was only obeying instructions. It cost a lot to run a place like this. She realized, with a slight shock, that her behaviour was very similar to the behaviour of the two guys in the pub. But for some reason she just couldn't abide this particular barman. She felt there was something slippery and underhand about him.

She opened her eyes and there he was, staring daggers across at her. She glared back at him. She felt that if each had a duelling pistol right then shots would be exchanged across the plush carpets of The Ranch.

Bert and Madge emerged from the dining room and came over to join her. Larry hadn't appeared and Bert had a sour look on his face.

"Larry must have been at the races," he announced. "That crowd behind us were at Mallow."

"Pity they didn't stay there," Linda remarked.

"They were inclined to be loud, all right," Bert agreed. "They must have won money. Here," he said, "we'll have one for the road. What'll it be?"

"I'm alright," Linda said, indicating the water.

"Are you sure?"

"Yes."

"I'll have a Bacardi and Coke, please," Madge requested.

"I think I'll stick with the Scotch an' soda," Bert decided.

Bert crossed to the bar.

"Are you enjoying yourself?" Madge asked.

"Yeah, everything is great," Linda lied.

"The meal was smashing, wasn't it?"

"Delicious."

"The desert was absolutely fabulous. You know, I think it was the best part of the whole meal. Bert downed yours."

"It looked nice."

"You should have indulged. Sure you have a great figure. You don't have to worry about losing weight." She put her hand to her midriff. "I feel as full as a tick."

No wonder, Linda thought. After all that food plus practically a full bottle of wine each. In the bar mirror she observed Bert being served. No money changed hands, however. Bert merely gave Bruno a smile, a nod and a wink. Maybe Bert did him a favour too. Bert must be a very generous man. Bert returned, transporting the small bottle of soda water in his top pocket. Bert and Madge must have been slightly tipsy at this stage, Linda reckoned. Bert's girth meant that his belt had no support from his hips and his trousers kept slipping down. They talked

86

away for about another twenty minutes—at least Bert and Madge cooed away like two lovebirds.

"If I was held up now I'd be over the limit," Bert stated the blatantly obvious as they got into the car and he prepared to drive. "But did you ever hear of one cop summonsing another cop for being over the limit? Heh, heh, heh!" he laughed, "Sure you have to have little perks in every job."

They arrived back safely in Cahir. Linda suggested that she'd wait in Madge's car and allow them a few minutes privacy before they headed back for Limerick. The few minutes turned out to be close to half an hour

"Will this bloody night ever end?" Linda hissed through gritted teeth. She had the window rolled down and eventually she heard the doors slam.

She heard Bert say, "I love you."

Madge said, "I do too."

Did Madge's reply mean that she actually loved herself, or was it Bert? How could any woman love Bert?

He came down to the car and said, "Safe journey. Take it easy."

"You're great to drive," Madge said as she clambered in.

"I like driving."

"We had a great night, hadn't we?" Madge commented, as they drove out of the town.

"It was enjoyable," Linda lied again. Inwardly she vehemently decided *never again.*

"I know it would have been more enjoyable for you if you had a man with you too."

"How do you know that, Madge?" Linda felt like asking.

"The next time we'll get one of Bert's colleagues to come along."

The horror of the suggestion caused Linda to smile to herself. Oh Jesus, wouldn't that be something! Especially if he turned out to be another Bert. What a whale of a time they'd all have then. It was a nice clear night for driving. She turned on the radio as this was the hour for her favourite music programme. They passed through Tipperary town and the straight road to Limerick loomed ahead. Madge had gone very quiet and she appeared to be asleep.

"Bert is very fat, for a guard." she suddenly said, out of the blue.

"He's a bit overweight, all right. It's probably not the best for his health, maybe."

After another few minutes, Madge said, "And he has B.O. Did you notice that?"

"Slightly," Linda replied, feeling completely surprised by this twist to the conversation.

Madge then went silent and Linda felt she was dozing off again. The drink, maybe, was getting her to say things. Then after a further ten minutes or so Linda got another surprise—shock might be closer to the mark—she felt Madge's hand above her knee, moving up and down her thigh. Linda didn't mind this. She rather enjoyed it, the same as a dog enjoys having his head and neck petted and rubbed.

Madge suddenly straightened bolt upright. "Oh God, Linda, I'm sorry, I'm sorry. What am I doing? I dozed off. I'm sorry. God, I'm awful sorry."

"It's all right, it's okay, don't worry."

"Are you sure?"

"Yes, I'm positive."

"I feel like kicking myself now."

"Don't."

A Tale of the Macabre

There was a strange and rather bizarre consequence to the previous tale: after a short period of time Bert and Madge duly married. But the marriage turned out to be a brief disaster that lasted a mere ten days. The net result was that Bert started to drink and gamble to an even greater extent than heretofore. He became a driven man, desperate for more and more money. Late at night he started to spy on cars outside pubs, followed the half-drunk drivers, pulled them over and demanded money in exchange for leniency.

As the result of a hunch he conducted a covert investigation into Larry's former lifestyle. He excitedly concluded that at last he had got a big break: He discovered some extraordinary dark secrets about his erstwhile friend's criminal past. Larry had spent five years as a guest of Her Majesty in Brixton prison. The long arm of the British jurisdiction was again reaching out for Larry, but Bert concluded that Larry probably felt safe enough in Cahir. There were serious question marks over how he had obtained the money to purchase The Ranch. If those stark facts were made known to the general public then Larry's business would, he knew, sink quicker than the *Titanic*. Bert confronted Larry and made it plain that his silence regarding those devastating revelations was worth a monetary reward. Larry remained in a state of shock for a number of days. From there on the more Bert lost to his gambling addiction the more he put the squeeze on Larry.

In the meantime the recession had hit business at The Ranch in a big way: the number of horses grazing in the paddocks had started to dwindle; pot-holes pock-marked the grand entrance; lawns were uncut; staff were let go; the catering and bar-trade trickled away to zero; guests were a rarity. Larry was starting to become demented. On top of everything else Bert was bleeding him dry. To survive some drastic action would need to be undertaken.

Bruno displayed his loyalty in a most magnanimous fashion: he offered his services for little or no reward until business picked up again. He was happy at The Ranch with his comfortable room and excellent food. And—most important to Bruno—Larry treated him with respect. Larry appreciated Bruno's kind gesture. In fact, Bruno became indispensable. He had a natural, ingrained ability with his hands, and he became the hotel plumber, electrician and mechanic. Bruno was chiefly responsible for keeping the hotel afloat through those lean, tough times. Larry and Bruno felt a bond rise up between them. They became very close. Larry confided to Bruno about his somewhat troubled, violent past, and what was now happening with Bert. His fear of being re-arrested. They had an alcohol fuelled tête-à-tête where their mutual past transgressions were resurrected. It transpired that Bruno, also, had to make a quick exit from Spain.

Between them, they hatched a plan to take care of Bert. Without realizing it, Bert was now skating on very thin ice. Pretty soon Bert telephoned Larry again, saying he needed two thousand euro in a bad way. Money lenders were threatening him. But Bert had used that ply a few times already. Was he starting to get careless and over-confident? Larry replied that he didn't have that much cash—it had to be cash—but he'd see what he could do. He suggested that Bert call along to The Ranch after his late night roster on Tuesday night, which usually ended at 2:30am. Bert agreed. Tuesday night was always the quietest night and the place was bound to be deserted at that late hour. At the appointed time Bert arrived along. Larry greeted him with a large Scotch.

Larry was careful not to sound any different than usual. He informed Bert that this whole thing would have to stop. Bert agreed, but Larry knew he had no intention of stopping. In about two weeks time the phone would ring again with a similar demand. Larry asked Bert *did he realize the state the country was in?* Hotels were going into liquidation all over the place.

"I'm sorry," Bert said. "But Christ I need the money. My life could hinge on it."

"I have some money hidden above in the bridal suite," Larry said. "I don't know exactly how much. Come on up and we'll see."

Bert followed Larry up the short flight of stairs, down the corridor to number ten—the bridal suite. They went inside. There was a small table with a single chair in the middle of the room. Larry motioned for Bert to be seated. Bert sat down with his back to the windows. Larry rummaged in a drawer, took out a brown envelope, pulled across a chair and sat facing Bert.

"You'll have me broke soon," Larry said. "I'm sorry now I ever heard of this place."

"Don't be like that," Bert said. "One of these days I'll settle with you. You can rest assured."

"You're going to win the lotto, Bert, are you?"

"I have other plans."

"You're having a bad run with the gee-gees, apparently?

"Rotten luck. Couldn't be worse."

"Here we are then," Larry said, starting to count out fifties.

The full-length curtains in front of one of the windows moved back and Bruno stood framed there. To distract Bert further, Larry said, "Fairy Dancer is going to win the three o'clock tomorrow at Roscommon."

"You're confident of that, are you? You got him good?" Bert inquired further, all ears.

"The trainer told me himself. You could hardly get it better than that." Bruno had crept up behind Bert. "He's what you'd call a racing certainty."

"He's worth a good cut?"

"You could put the whole lot there on him. How much have we?"

"Show me," Bert said, reaching out for the money.

It was the last act he ever performed, for, with a mighty swipe, Bruno sank a lump hammer into Bert's skull. Death was instantaneous.

Quickly searching Bert's pocket, Bruno located the keys to the patrol car. They then quickly wrapped Bert's remains in a black plastic sheet they had pre-arranged for the purpose. They half-carried, half-dragged Bert's lifeless form across and tumbled him into the bath of the nearby en-suite. Bert proved heavier dead than he looked alive.

Bruno put on his gloves, went out, looked carefully about, got into the patrol car and drove back down the gravelled avenue, turned in a gateway, crossed two fields and parked the car beside the river Suir. He left the driver's door open and threw the keys out into the water. He then made his way back, cross country, to the hotel.

Larry and Bruno were both avid fans of the television series *The Sopranos*. They recorded each programme and viewed it together when the bar closed. In one particularly gruesome episode Tony Soprano and his vicious, volatile, psychotic nephew Christopher stripped naked and systematically dismembered a body in a bath. Larry and Bruno had decided to adopt the same procedure with Bert.

They removed their clothes and spent the next few hours stripping the flesh from Bert's body. This they deposited into black plastic bags that they later stored in the hotel's deep freezer. Bert's internal organs, his skeletal remains, his shoes and clothes they wrapped in the plastic sheeting and flung the lot into the fully turned up, blazing furnace of the hotel's heating system. They then cleaned everything thoroughly, stood under the shower for a considerable length of time, dressed, adjourned to the bar and treated themselves to a stiff drink.

It was now 7:30am.

Bert's 'suicide' created a sensation in Cahir and its surrounds. Various theories were bandied about: the wife left him and he was depressed... She's a real hussy, that one... Sure everyone knew what he was like—he took bribes... There was an internal Garda inquiry being conducted into his activities... The noose was tightening... He was going to be dismissed from the force in disgrace... It wasn't suicide at all—it was a drugs gang that got rid of him. It's a wonder his body wasn't found though, but then the river was in spate and he could be washed all the way down to the sea.

Nothing lasts forever. The worst of the recession was behind. Trade slowly started to pick up at The Ranch. Then it started to accelerate rapidly. The sun started to shine again, the rose garden went into bloom, the lawns were trimmed, the horses frolicked in the lush meadows once more. The smile returned to Larry's face. Bruno had managerial status now and with a beaming face he happily mingled with the satisfied revellers.

Larry and Bruno decided to host a large banquet on New Year's Eve. The event was booked out well in advance. The night arrived and a sumptuous time was being enjoyed by all. The music was excellent and the alcohol flowed like water. Food was there in abundance.

The main course consisted of the following choice:

Golden vale sirloin
Wild Atlantic salmon
The Ranch stew de Magnifique

For a touch of variety most diners opted for the stew de Magnifique—the last mortal remains of Bert. The new chef had done a marvellous job. The black plastic bags had been removed from the freezer and deposited into a large cauldron.

At first the chef didn't like the odour, but he soon disguised this little problem by using a whole range of spices and herbs. He mixed in a multitude of seasonal vegetables. He then added ginger, salt, peppers, chilli, garlic and curry, so that the finished product, as it bubbled away, gave off an irresistible aroma. In fact, everyone agreed that the stew was truly magnificent. Bert, himself, would have been proud of it.

Madge attended this gala evening, as she did any event of consequence being launched in the area. She had moved down to Cahir at this stage. As she chewed away on a part of Bert's upper thigh she remarked to her current buxom partner that the meat was very succulent. There may not have been much intimacy in Madge and Bert's marriage, but at that particular moment of time could any two people be closer?

Wasteland

The sun now it shines on the green fields of France,
There's a warm summer breeze that makes the red poppies dance,
And look how the sun shines from under the trees,
There's no gas, no barbed wire, there's no guns firing now.

Billy O'Neill has just turned nineteen. He is a fit, strong, country youth who was born and reared in Ardfinnan, Co. Tipperary. Today is a big day in his young life. After conducting four weeks of initial training at the military barracks in Clonmel he was allowed home yesterday to bid farewell to his family. The month is March and the year is 1915. Billy has joined the Royal Irish Regiment. Tomorrow, with the rest of his battalion, he will be on his way to Aldershot in England. He finds the excitement of the whole adventure overwhelming. He was never very far from home in his whole life. Ken Ryan, from a small farm outside the village, enlisted the same time as himself. Billy is walking down the narrow lane to the road, where he is to meet up with Ken. Both will then be transported to Clonmel by ken's father, in the pony and trap.

The previous evening Billy had spent a few hours with his young sweetheart, Maggie Keane. She was a soft hearted, doe-eyed, innocent girl. She said she'd pray for him every day that he'd return safely to her. She gave him a special prayer, sealed in a little leather cover. She made him promise that he'd keep it with him always. It would protect him. They walked down by the river, stood under a tree, kissed and cuddled. He felt her soft tears against his cheeks. More tears as they kissed goodbye. She said she wouldn't go to see him off tomorrow. She couldn't bear that part of it.

Billy's mother Annie, his father, Pakie, and his six siblings join him, as he walks down the little lane. They are dressed in rags as the family is extremely poor. Billy's father works as a farm labourer for a shilling and four pence a week All are talking excitedly now. They are proud of Billy, he looks such a fine cut of a lad in his smart uniform. They become aware of the pony and trap approaching in the distance.

The mood changes. Tears well up in Annie's eyes and she commences to sob, as do the two oldest girls. Pakie is overcome—he pats Billy on the shoulder a few times, turns round and walks back towards the house. He doesn't want the others to see the tears running down his cheeks. The pony halts. Greetings are exchanged. Annie hugs Billy, as do the girls. All are crying openly now. The two older boys shake Billy's hand, saying. "Good-luck, Billy." The two little girls, with the pinched hungry faces, wrap their hands round Billy's legs, not wanting him to go.

"Take care of yourself, Billy boy," Annie says, "and may God look after you."

"It's all right, it's all right," Billy reassures them, "I'll be home by Christmas." He extricates the little ones' hands and heaves himself up to the sanctuary of the trap.

Billy is struggling hard to contain his emotions. But on no account could he cry in front of Ken or his father, Jim. Grown men don't cry in public—especially soldiers.

"Git up there, Jilly," Jim says "And good-luck to you all."

Jilly sets off at a lively clip. All wave goodbye once more.

"Parting is always the hardest," Jim says.

Billy looks back at the dishevelled, ragged appearance of the warm, closely knit family he loved so much.

By pony and trap was a lovely way to travel. Scenery could be appreciated and admired at leisure. Jilly, the beautiful roan pony knew this road well. Jim allowed Jilly to travel at her own pace. He had a great fondness for this pony. Everyone had.

"When will we travel this road again?" Ken wonders aloud.

"Everyone says it should be over soon," Billy replies.

"I'd say it will; it won't last too long more," Jim says with conviction. "The British Empire, France, Russia—too many big powers on the one side."

"I hope it won't be over before we get there," Ken worries. "I just can't wait."

"We'll see a bit of the world. We'll have some stories to tell when we get back," Billy states with glee.

"Learn to keep your heads down and don't be acting the heroes, that's my advice to you," Jim warns.

Halfway to Clonmel they halt to give the pony a brief rest. Jim has a nosebag with oats in the trap which he now drapes over Jilly's head. She munches away on the oats. Ken opens a small parcel. He hands Billy a bottle of lemonade and takes one himself. Jim accepts and uncorks a bottle of stout. Ken passes around sandwiches. Billy thanks him, thinking to himself that this was a nice gesture.

They eventually get to Clonmel and cross the old bridge leading to the main section of the town. They hear rousing marching music and see people standing on the footpaths. They pull over to a little green patch, get out and go to have a look. The army is on parade and getting nearer. Billy's nerves tingle with excitement. An officer mounted on a grey horse leads the parade, followed by the brass band, the colour party and the ranks of marching soldiers. It is an impressive and glorious sight. The onlookers applaud and clap their hands. Perhaps it was meant as a recruitment drive—whatever, it was a memory to cherish.

Getting near their destination, Billy says he'll hop out and give the others the privacy to say their goodbyes. He thanks Jim, who in turn wishes Billy the best of luck, telling him to take good care of himself. It isn't long before the two friends are reunited and they enter the military barracks together. What an adventure awaits them now. The significance of it all is taking time to register. Going overseas. Going off to war. Isn't it what the clergy and politicians are urging men like Billy to do? Go and fight for the freedom of small nations. Fight for little Catholic Belgium.

On to Queenstown by rail, and then by boat to Liverpool. Billy and Ken are fascinated by all the new things they are now experiencing. They were never on a ship before. A crewman tells them that there is always the danger of the ship being torpedoed. The German U-boats are creating havoc. Ken gets seasick. "Christ I'm dying," he says, his face turning green. Then the final trek of their journey, on to Aldershot. Ardfinnan seems a long way off now. The masses of military men everywhere, all preparing to embark for France. The war is on everyone's lips. Nobody speaks about anything else. Ken has a black eye. He had a fistfight with a Dubliner who called him a thick, ignorant, country bogman.

The Sergeant Major is a tough nut. The physical training is turning out to be fierce, the hardest Billy ever endured. The drill on the square, the forced marching through the surrounding countryside weighed down with heavy kit, the endurance course, the crawling under barbed wire, everything to toughen the new recruits. Everything to toughen them for the inevitable apocalypse into which they would soon be heading. Billy and Ken enjoy the rifle training. Firing their .303 rifles at targets. This was more like it. Then the bayonet practice. Billy experiences a slight shiver as he feels the sharp, sleek, cold steel and realizes what it was actually meant to do. They scream as they charge at hanging bags of sand and plunge the bayonets home.

"No mercy!" the Sergeant Major roars. "Show no mercy for no mercy will be shown to you. You will soon be on your way. We've done all we could to prepare you. I hope your bodies are hardened by now. I want your minds to be hardened too. The enemy you will soon be facing is a tough, dangerous foe. You will have to be just as tough and uncompromising as he is. For if you don't," he roars, "you will be a dead soldier. Remember that, always remember that."

Disturbing rumours are soon circulating: where the troops are going is no cakewalk. The Western Front is an awful place. If there was a hell on earth then it would be the nearest thing to it. Those readying themselves to go try to ignore these reports, convincing themselves that it couldn't be that bad. The band play them off to war. The spectators cheer. Girls dash across and plant kisses on their cheeks and flowers in their buttonholes. They all feel like heroes.

If Billy and Ken had any doubts, when they finally

reach their destination their worst fears are confirmed. This, they quickly realize, is indeed an awful place. The first thing they notice on their way to the frontline is the smell—rotting bodies in shallow graves, men who haven't washed for weeks because there are no facilities, overflowing cess pits, chloride of lime used to stave off infection, cordite, the stagnant mud everywhere. In the trenches they soon become aware that rats are a constant companion. They are there in millions, everywhere, gorging themselves on human remains. They grow to the size of cats. Lice become a big problem, breeding on dirty clothes. Then the constant wet and cold. They were warned that the mud and unsanitary conditions could cause trench foot which could turn gangrenous and require amputation. A sizable number of men appeared to be suffering from shell shock. It was brought starkly home to the new arrivals that death was everywhere in the trenches—at any time, day or night, it could be your body lying in the mud. Horrified at finding themselves in this hellhole, Billy and Ken resign themselves to the grim reality that they had no choice now.

The days started off before dawn with 'stand to.' Men were roused from whatever fitful sleep they had got and ordered to the 'fire step.' Many raids were carried out at dawn. After 'stand to' there was an inspection of men and rifles by a senior officer.

After that there was a breakfast of sorts. The trenches came alive after dark as men fetched vital food and supplies from behind the lines. Canned corn beef was the staple diet. Six ounces of meat and six ounces of vegetables was the daily allowance. This was eventually replaced by pea soup and a few lumps of horse meat.

Billy and Ken are getting conditioned to the rifle

fire and shelling. Then the action slows somewhat. It appears as if the second battle of Ypres is about to end in stalemate. Suddenly a lot of activity is observed in the opposing trenches. The troops are put on full alert. The Germans made a habit of attacking in force when it was least expected. Being countrymen and familiar with horses, Billy and Ken are sent with a convoy to collect supplies from behind the lines. The area is subjected to a heavy barrage and they are forced to remain overnight, not returning to their position till the next day. As they approach they become aware of a strange, foul odour. They had already witnessed some atrocious sights but what confronts them now is the worst horror they have ever seen: The first poison gas attack of the war has taken place. Caught unawares, there are hundreds, thousands, of dead and dying soldiers all along the line. Ashen faced, shocked, they watch soldiers spitting, suffocating, twisted in mortal fear, their faces turning blue while they cough out mucus and blood from their tortured lungs.

The war wages on seemingly unending. The gas is now the greatest dread. It was now a feared weapon on both sides. Billy finds it impossible to get used to the suffering and screams and blood of Flanders. Seeing the remains of men shattered by shell blast. Seeing the flower of youth sent to death and mutilation. Ken has been moved to a different sector and both hope the other will survive. Survival is all the soldiers have to aim for now.

Word filters through about the Easter Rising in Dublin in 1916. The troops can't believe it. It's like a dagger to the heart. British and Irishmen shooting each other on the streets of Dublin! How could it happen? Then a couple of weeks later news leaks about the executions of the leaders of the Rebellion. Another mind numbing shock, tinged with anger now. Attitudes change. *What are we doing here?* a lot of men question.

"How could the army be so stupid?" Dublin Danny fumes. "How could they?"

Straight away, the comradeship between the soldiers from the North and South cools or, in some instances, evaporates completely. A month later Dublin Danny goes home on furlough. Eventually when he gets back he reports that everything has changed utterly at home:

"You'd be despised now if you were seen wearing khaki. We're not wanted back in Ireland anymore," he sadly declares.

"What are we going to do then?" Billy asks in total despair.

"What are we going to do? We'll have to stick this basterin' nightmare out. What else can we do?"

"They all urged us to join, to enlist, to come out here," Tom Griffin from Wexford spits out. "They fuckin' sent us out here. Now they don't want us back."

"I'll tell you what we are now—we're the damned generation, that's what we are," Dublin Danny adds with a finality to his voice.

Billy's leave is due. He decides he won't go home now. He might bring trouble down on the heads of his family. He'll spend it somewhere in France. He'll try and write a letter home later on. He does so, in his scrawly hand:

Hallo Mam and Dad and everyone,
I hope this finds you all well. Sorry I did not rite before now but I am not into letters. Do not worry about me at all as I will be al right. I think of you all the hole time. Maggie is always in my toughts. I am sending you six pound. Keep the fiver to buy someting for

everyone when Xmas comes round. Give the pound
to Maggie and tell her to buy someting nice to wear. I
will not rite again. I am no good at it. I pray that I will
see you all very soon. I love you all and miss you all
very much. I think of you first thing at morning and
last thing at night. Give my dearist love to Maggie.
Your loving son,
Billy.

The war of attrition rumbles on. After seven months Ken is reunited with his old regiment. The psychological impact of the trench warfare is taking its toll on both Billy and Ken. Both look as if they have aged about a dozen years. Their faces have an intense, gaunt appearance. Ken relates a particularly bad experience he had about a month previous: a shell burst close and part of a comrade's head and brains splashed onto his face. Billy too had a brush with sudden death, when a shell smashed into the wall of the trench close to where he was crouched. It didn't explode but buried itself in the soft salient of Flanders earth. Some thirty per cent of the shells fired by both sides failed to explode.

In July 1917 a huge push is planned at Passendaele. This is to be the big breakthrough that will finally break the back of the German army. All the troops that can be mustered are rushed to the front—over a large area, close to the town of Passendaele. For days and nights the guns pound the enemy lines. Over four million shells blast the German positions. It starts to rain incessantly. For the soldiers waiting in the trenches, conditions couldn't be much worse. The trenches start to fill with water. The clinging mud is everywhere. That, and the rats. The rats bore through corpses to get at the liver. Billy peers over the parapet at the bombardment.

"How could the Germans survive that!" he murmurs to Ken in awe. "How could they?"

But he knew that they would, the same as at the Somme and elsewhere. They'd dig deep underground.

"The constant explosions must be driving them out of their minds," Ken surmises. "It's bound to drive men mad."

The bombardment goes on and on. At night the flames from the shells lights up the night sky. When the soldiers open their eyes at morning they feel paralysed with the wet and cold. When Billy looks down the line, what he sees is hulks of men moulded in mud from head to toe. He looks out at no man's land, that zone of terror, that awful place where the moans of dying men never seem to cease. Billy knows what is coming next: the shelling will halt, the Germans will drag themselves up from the bowels of the earth, position their machine guns and destroy the oncoming waves of British infantry. He is well aware of the casual way the generals dispatch wave after wave of brave men on suicidal missions—mindless squandering of human life for negligible results. At last the fatal word comes through—the shelling will cease next morning.

A long night stretches out—the long wait. Reinforcements arrive all along the frontline trenches. It will be a big assault—a crucial battle, maybe. Nerves are frayed all night as the troops wait for the dawn—the last dawn for a great number. With shaking hands some men scribble letters, some pray more than usual, all are secretly terrified. The shelling stops abruptly. The first advance will go over the top at 7am sharp. Billy and Ken keep close together.

"Why the bloody wait?" Billy asks, with disgust "It's

only giving them more time to prepare. Look, feckin' barbed-wire everywhere."

A nerve shattering stillness now engulfs the whole theatre of war.

The rain has stopped pelting down. The men are at the ready. The order to fix bayonets is shouted out. The rum is being distributed. Father O'Mahony makes his way along through the mud administering a general absolution. The vast majority of the men, including Billy and Ken, remove their helmets and reverently bow their heads as he blesses them. Some don't bother. Hell doesn't worry them. They feel they have lived through it. The priest was a good one. He stuck with the men through thick and thin. He looked haggard and tired. A crazed looking officer with a revolver in his hand is pacing up and down the trench screaming, "Kill! Kill! Show no mercy!"

Glancing left and right Billy notices a few men getting sick and vomiting. More are kissing some personal religious icon. Others are glancing down at faded photographs. All are aware that the next few minutes could be their last few minutes on this earth. Billy feels his heart pounding inside his chest. He glances down at his watch— he had taken the watch from a dead German's wrist. It was the only item he ever took from a dead body. What difference, he reasoned at the time. It would be ruined anyway. It kept good time. One minute to go. Pale-faced, Ken reaches over saying, 'Good-luck.' Billy nods his head.

The whistles sound. Screams and curses rent the air as the men scramble up the wooden ladders and over the top. They rush towards the enemy lines and straight away the deadly rattle of the German machine guns open up. Men start to drop like flies, like corn before the scythe. Everywhere the agonized screams of the wounded are heard as bullets thud home, the heavy machine gun bullets shattering flesh and bone.

Keeping low and dodging in and out of shell holes, Billy gets close to the German line. The attacking soldiers are now starting to hurtle grenades at the defending Germans. Sheer force of numbers is forcing the Germans to retreat. In the smoke and confusion, Billy sees a figure come towards him. Instinctively he lunges forward and plunges his bayonet into the German's chest. Straight away Billy realizes that the soldier is unarmed. Mortally wounded, he slumps to the ground. As Billy looks down in shock he can see that his victim is only a youth—a boy. The helmet comes off and the blond hair falls down over his forehead. He looks up at Billy as his life ebbs away. Billy tries to pull out the bayonet, but he can't—it's stuck in bone. He has to put his boot on the boy's chest to yank out the weapon. As he does so blood oozes out of the corners of the boy's mouth. Billy recoils in horror. He is shoved and pushed from behind and in a turbulent, shocked state of mind he stumbles forward and collapses into the now undefended trench.

The adrenalin is pumping in the men who have also made it to safety. Some are doubled up now, panting for breath. There are a number of dead Germans slumped about in the blood stained mud—the ones who had fought to the bitter end. A small number have surrendered and they are huddled about in a frightened cluster, looking every bit as wretched as their captors. It was a victory of sorts for the attacking forces, but at what a cost.

Ken, too, has survived the deadly German fire. He seeks Billy out and eventually finds him, sitting alone, weeping bitter tears into his hands.

"I killed an unarmed German boy of about sixteen."

Billy had heard of pacifists, the ones who would rather die themselves than kill another human being. He is now convinced that the young dead German soldier was one of them. Ken tries to console Billy.

"Anything can happen in the heat of battle. It's you or them. Christ, that's the way it is. Don't worry about it."

But Billy is inconsolable. He is caught up in an overwhelming, terrible, guilt-ridden, black depression.

"The way he looked up at me—there was no hatred in his eyes. He looked as if… as if he even wanted to forgive me. Oh Jesus help me," he cries in anguish. "What have I done? I murdered him."

Over the next few days there are sporadic attacks. The men work furiously to repair the trench, and start digging another back to the support line. Apart from Ken, Billy has given up conversing with the other men. The image of the dead German youth is constantly on his mind. It haunts him day and night. Ken is now concerned about Billy's mental health. Tough Sergeant Sweeney—Swearin' Sweeney—from Carlow comes along.

"Keep your fuckin' heads down," he barks to no-one in particular. Don't you know there are deadly fuckin' snipers out there."

He calls Ken to one side.

"What's fuckin' wrong with him?" he asks Ken, "Could he be shell-shocked, do you think?"

"I'd say he could be."

"I'll get someone to have a fuckin' look at him. In the meantime keep an eye on him, will yah? Keep a fuckin' eye on him."

"I will, Sergeant."

Sergeant Sweeney shuffles off. Ken rejoins Billy.

"Remember the day we travelled by pony and trap

to Clonmel," Ken reminds Billy. "It was a lovely peaceful day."

"It feels like a hundred years ago," Billy weakly responds.

"Little did we know then what we were in for. Billy, we've come through a lot together. This thing will have to end soon. I don't want anything to happen to us now. You hear me?"

There is a pause, then Billy suddenly says: "Ken, are your clothes dry?"

"Yeah, I'm dry enough—the top part of me anyhow."

"Will you keep this for me?" He passes over the little leather covered prayer he got from Maggie.

"That's what you got from Maggie, isn't it? The prayer?"

"Yeah, that's it."

"Can I look at it?"

"Sure, look away. It'll keep you safe."

Ken takes the prayer, turns sideways to avail of the light and reads:

> *Dear Jesus, please look after me this day,*
> *And take me safely home from the road I now travel,*
> *This treacherous road that is so fraught with danger,*
> *My Dearest Jesus I place all my trust in Thee,*
> *And when this life's journey is finally over,*
> *May my soul rest for all eternity in peace with You.*

He turns back "It's nice—oh Christ!"

Billy is half-way up the side of the trench. Jumping forward, Ken grabs him by the legs but he knows it is too late—he has heard the crack of the rifle. Ken slides back in despair, his hands clasping Billy's limp form.

*

Annie is hanging out the laundry. Washing the clothes for so many is a constant chore. She notices Maggie hurrying up the lane. She goes out to meet her. Maggie is in a distressed state and she runs and throws her arms around Annie.

"Oh Annie," she says, "I had an awful dream last night. I dreamt Billy was dead. It was all so real, so very real."

Annie comforts her: "No, he's not dead. Don't be thinking like that, upsetting yourself. You'll see, he'll come back safely to us." She points, "Some day we'll look down the lane and there he'll be. Smiling, he'll throw his arms wide and he'll run up and embrace the two of us." She hugs Maggie close. "Hush now love, hush."

Now, Willie McBride, I can't help wonder why,
Do all those who lie here know why did they die?
And did they really believe when they answered the call,
Did they really believe that this war would end wars?
THE FUREYS AND DAVEY ARTHUR, *The Green Fields Of France*

The Golden Slipper

The Golden Slipper was a dancehall built on the outskirts of the town, the property of Mister McNabb, a prominent local business man, who saw it as a means of generating more money to add to his already considerable fortune. The Golden Slipper was nothing more than a glorified shed, built on the cheap, painted in a gaudy yellow. The maple dance-floor was the dearest part of the construction. The dancing arena was approached through a hallway containing the ticket office and cloakrooms. The dancefloor was surrounded by a walkway with seating along by the walls. The place had a ladies' and gents' toilet. There was a mineral bar adjacent to the dancing area, entered through an archway. Also in evidence was a changing room for the band at the back of the stage. Next to this was situated a small kitchen-cum-office where Mr McNabb counted the night's takings. The sale of alcoholic drink was prohibited by law, except on special occasions. Mr McNabb compensated for this by charging double for the minerals.

Hacker lived a few miles outside the town. He was standing outside the gateway admiring his new purchase—a second-hand Ford Prefect. Cars were only gradually becoming available back in 1954. Due to the economic situation at the time most families couldn't afford the purchase price. Hacker, however, felt he had got the car at a bargain price as the former owner was joining thousands of others in taking the emigrant ship. He felt over the moon with this car as he couldn't remember all the times he got drenched cycling home from town on the bike. He had his night planned in advance: He'd go to the dance later on but first he'd spend an hour or two in Lanigan's pub. He'd like to get a bit oiled first without getting plastered completely. The birds can be particular. He wiped a bit of dust off the side of the car with a rag and walked around it again. He looked under the seats and found a half-crown. He spat on it for luck.

Margo, Alice and Eileen were standing at the cross-roads waiting for the hackney car that would take them to the dance in town. They did this on a regular basis. As the three girls lived close by, and if the evening was pleasant, they liked to meet up and stroll down to the cross-roads. If it happened to be raining then Mossie Dourney, the hackney driver, called to each house separately.

They discussed the various men they were likely to dance with during the coming night. The same crowd, more or less, attended the Friday night dances. Entertainment, generally, was pretty restricted in the fifties. Girls frequenting bars was unheard of back then. It was either the dancehall or the picture house. Films like *The Adventures of Old Mother Riley, Lassie Come Home, Heidi,* and *Francis the Talking Mule,* were the types on offer. There were strict censorship laws and any film portraying sex in any shape or form was taboo. Stories floated about, and the pedigree of various men was discussed and dissected. The girls agreed that certain men were to be avoided at all costs. They were only after the 'one thing.' Hacker's name came up. Alice and Eileen teased Margo, saying he had his eye on her. Margo dismissed this out of hand, but at the same time she had to admit to herself that she liked dancing with him. However, she had her suspicions about whether she could trust him or not.

"The truth is, the three of us are stuck unless we meet some fella with transport," Alice said. "Did Hacker offer to drive you home on the bar of the bike yet?" she joked.

The girls enjoyed a cigarette as they waited. Mossie was a bit on the late side. They didn't mind as the evening was warm and balmy. They wondered aloud about what condition Mossie would be in—especially on the return trip home. He was often under the weather and they laughed about some hair-raising experiences they'd had in the past. There was little danger involved though, as Mossie never exceeded thirty miles-an-hour.

Three weeks previous he was 'well on' coming home—there had been heavy rain and he took a corner too wide and drove up on the soft margin. The wheels started to skid and the girls had to get out and push. The spinning back tyres destroyed the girls' dresses with mud. Eileen lost one of her shoes in the squelching soil. They laughed hysterically in the back of the car for the rest of the journey home. Mossie, a small man, offered Eileen a loan of one of his shoes as she said the entrance to her house was rough and stony. Out of 'divilment' Eileen took the shoe.

"He's coming!" Margo shouted to Alice who had hopped over the gateway and was picking and eating a few juicy blackberries. The car pulled up and turned round. Greetings were exchanged as the three girls piled in. He appeared sober. As they drove along Alice asked Mossie how the gout was.

"I have only the slight touch of it now, but begod I was crippled last Friday night. "Tis a fierce sore complaint."

"Too much high living, Mossie," Eileen ventured.

"Too much low livin' would be nearer the mark. Times are tough, girl. No two ways about it."

The girls knew what their itinerary for the evening would be: they'd arrive in town a bit too early to go to the dance so they'd amble around the few streets looking at the jewellers and the clothes-shop windows, then they'd go in to the little cake shop and treat themselves to a cup of tea and a cream bun. They'd take their time but still arrive at the dancehall early. They'd sit back, listen to the music, smoke a cigarette and watch the ones who considered themselves expert ballroom dancers swan around—the ones with the stiff backs and tilted heads enjoying the empty spaces before the common herd arrived.

Hacker had driven uneventfully into town. The engine did a bit of 'hegging' before it started up so he assumed the battery was low. He decided to park it facing down a hill. He'd feel a right idiot if he picked up a bird and the car wouldn't start. He'd go to the dance later on, but first he'd have a few drinks at Lanigan's pub. Entering the premises he soon joined up with a few cronies—Jim, Mick and Toddy. In conjunction with buying rounds of drink they started to play games of darts. All were members of the John Mitchell Slashers GAA club.

The GAA is the commonly used abbreviation for Gaelic Athletic Association. Back in those days, and for a considerable number of years afterwards, the GAA had a strange rule on their statute books: it meant that their playing members were prohibited from watching or supporting soccer, rugby or cricket. Members were also prohibited from attending social functions organised by such clubs. This rule was universally known as The Ban. It was a rule that was vigorously enforced—any errant players were subjected to lengthy suspensions. Certain committees were instigated to enforce 'The Ban.' These were known as The Vigilante Committees.

On this particular Friday night the dance was organized as a fund raising venture by the newly formed soccer club The Riverside Rovers. This was anathema to the officials of The Slashers. Mister O'Riann, secretary of the club, viewed it as an act of treason which had to be put down at all costs. The Vigilante Committee was quickly organised to monitor the attendance. True supporters of The Slashers were urged to keep away.

Jonny Lanigan, the proprietor of the pub, asked Hacker and his buddies were they going to the soccer dance.

"I'm going anyway," Toddy answered, "Are you going, Hacker?"

"God I am, yeah." Mick and Jim also confirmed their intention of attending.

"You'll be all suspended," Jonny added. "The Vigilante boys will be out in force tonight."

"The Vigilante boys can go to hell," Mick said. "They're not going to tell me what to do."

"Mister O'Cregain will be there," Jonny smiled mischievously.

"Mister O'Cregain wants a kick in the nuts. That would straighten him out," Jim stated. "And he might get it too—sooner than he thinks."

"You ought to be ashamed of yourselves," county councillor Sean MacToibin remarked. "Supporting foreign games. Have you any sense of history?"

"That's right," Seamus O'Cinneide, chairman of the local Fianna Fail cumann agreed with his friend. "That bloody soccer club should be run out of town."

Sean MacToibin and Seamus O'Cinneide were sitting together, hunched over a table, smoking and nursing their pints of Guinness. Both men were heavy-set, in their late fifties, with red faces, who rarely indulged in any form of exercise—apart from walking to and fro to Lanigan's.

"DeValera played rugby," Hacker reminded Seamus, winking at Toddy, having already spotted 'The Bark' Sullivan of Fine Gael.

"He might have," Seamus replied, taking the bait. "So did Kevin Barry. But that was before Mick Collins, the traitor, sold out the North."

From the far-off recesses of a dark corner of the pub, The Bark Sullivan roared, "Shut your mouth Kennedy, or I'll shut it for you! Look at the state your bloody crowd have the country in."

"What about the shilling your crowd took off the old-age pensioners?" Seamus O'Cinneide roared back.

"Remember the economic war?" The Bark replied in kind.

"Remember the Seventy-Seven?"

Jonny Lanigan thumped the counter "Enough of that now! You know the golden rule here—no talk of politics or religion." Silence reigned supreme for some seconds.

"You're right too," Mick said, concentrating on his dart throwing, "A pub is no place for politics or religion."

"Or vigilante committees," Jim added.

"Look at that—a bull!" Mick exclaimed.

"I'll tell you something for nothing," Toddy declared, "half last year's team are in England. If old Cregain wants a team he'd want to go over to Camden Town. Wait an' see, he'll be gettin' the bus driver to tog out again."

"Did you ever hear better!" Sean MacToibin uttered with disgust, chiefly to change the subject. "It's no wonder The Slashers can't win a match. A team of wasters who train in the pub. Making a laughing stock of us all—making a show of the whole town."

"You're forgetting the women, Sean—the young ones keep us fit," Mick grinned.

"Oh God help the young ones, that's all I have to say. When I look around me at the choice they have I'm only glad I haven't a daughter myself," Sean declared.

"You're dead right," Seamus as usual agreed. "And when I look around me I have to shake my head and wonder what the glorious men of 1916 died for."

"They'd turn in their graves," Sean lamented.

"Hey, Seamus," Hacker said, winking at his companions again, "your father was in a flying column, wasn't he?"

"Damn sure he was," Seamus stated proudly. "Out there on the side of a mountain, wet and hungry."

"He was hungry all right," The Bark shouted across "because the man never did a day's work in his life."

Seamus O'Cinneide sprang to his feet. "I don't have to stand here and listen to that yoke over there in the corner."

Jonny Lanigan banged the counter again.

At around eleven-thirty Hacker and company decided they'd head down to the dance. First each one bought two miniature bottles—Baby Powers—of whiskey, which they stuffed into their inside pockets. They took a small detour up the hill to have a look at Hacker's car. They complimented him on his purchase and continued towards the dancehall. The streets of the small town were mostly deserted, apart from a few other stragglers walking in the same direction as themselves. The only sign of life was in the other two pubs they passed on the way. A drunken man shuffled along the footpath, his hand against the wall for support. They felt slightly inebriated themselves, but had taken care not to over-indulge. As they approached the entrance to the dancehall they became aware of Mister O'Cregain, and a couple of others they couldn't make out, standing back in the shadows.

"Look at old Cregain," Jim remarked. "He have an eye like a hawk."

"He have an eye like a shithouse rat," Toddy added, for good measure.

"Ignore 'em—take no notice," Mick said.

They strode purposefully on, without glancing left or right. Aggie, Mr. McNabb's daughter, manned the small ticket office—this important function had to be conducted by a family member. Mr. McNabb would trust no outsider. 'Trust no-one and that way you won't be disappointed,' was an oft-used expression of his. Each paid the two shillings entry charge. Jackie the Leg was collecting the tickets at the door to the dancefloor itself.

"Many in?" Hacker asked casually.

"A goodish crowd, considering," Jackie the Leg answered, nodding his head towards the outside door.

"What's the talent like?" Mick asked.

"A fair sprinkling—you won't be disappointed."

The four entered the dancing area and stood at the back having a good look around. Toddy, the most dapper, ran a comb through his hair. The band playing was a local one, consisting of five local men. At the time some dance bands were starting to wear a distinctive type of uniform. The local outfit onstage favoured the cowboy look. They called themselves The Swinging Dixies. However, they were far better known around the town as The Swingin' Dickies. This was a turn of phrase used by men only. Mr. O'Cregain tried to get The Swingin' Dickies to pull out of their engagement with the soccer club. When they refused his demand he informed them that they'd never again play at a Slashers function.

Back in that era the bands earned their money the hard way, as the dances didn't end till around 3am. The usual format consisted of the band playing a session of three fast dances, the quickstep, followed by a session of three slow dances to the tempo of the slow waltz or the foxtrot. Sometimes, to add a touch of variety, they changed the tempo to the samba, or, as sometimes requested, an Irish ceilidh dance like *The Siege of Ennis* or *The Stack of Barley*. There was a lull between each three-dance sequence, when the girls moved to one side of the dancefloor and the men to the other. When the dance music recommenced there would be a slight stampede, as the men rushed across the floor to grab hold of their favourite partner before someone else got there first. In that era a girl never refused a request to dance unless the man was legless drunk.

There was a rather cruel aspect to this procedure in one respect: the unfortunate girls who weren't endowed with some form of natural beauty were often left standing, whilst the pretty ones were being asked out to dance right left and centre. The girls who were left standing there were called wallflowers. They just stood around, feeling miserable, their feelings hurt, watching the other dancers enjoy themselves. Worse still, they knew this humiliation would be repeated over and over. Sometimes, out of pity, a family friend or a girl's brother might ask her out to dance.

Every area, or small town, had a few peculiar—or strange—characters. One of those was Weird Willie. He attended the Friday night dances without fail. However, he never danced himself but took in every minute detail of the night's proceedings. He was renowned for casting vile aspersions at some of the dancers—especially the girls. Hacker, inadvertently, found himself standing next to Weird Willie who intoned in a solemn monotone, for Hacker's benefit that the fattish girl standing over by the pillar was supposed to be a great ride. In fact, the fattish girl standing over by the pillar was far more likely to be a member of The Legion of Mary.

"That so," Hacker replied. "Any more good things around, Willie?"

"Why are you asking me that, Hacker? Haven't you Susie."

"Susie's not like that. Susie is a decent girl."

"She is in my hole," Weird Willie responded, moving away, as some other item of interest caught his attention.

Susie had a flame burning for Hacker and he had walked her home a few times. They usually ended up in some quiet spot. He knew well that Susie was the best court he had ever met. The big downside was that a lot of people shared Weird Willie's perception of Susie's morals. Hacker resented the smart-ass comments at work about himself and Susie.

He decided he'd have to set his sights on someone else. He also realized that he wasn't getting any younger, so maybe it was time he started to take things serious. He had taken a fancy to Margo and knew her as a regular dance partner.

As he gazed about he quickly became aware that Margo and Susie were both in attendance. *This could be a bit tricky,* he concluded. The Swingin' Dickies were going hell for leather. Their white shirts were stained with sweat.

Margo, Alice and Eileen were in high demand, on the floor for every dance. They decided they'd sit one out and have a rest and a smoke.

They moved back to the seats by the wall.

"How are you getting on?" Margo asked.

"That Lar Hennessy is pestering me the whole time," Eileen said. "He's over like a flash for every dance. What am I going to tell him? I can't keep dancing with that idiot all night. Did you see the cut of him?"

The other two laughed.

"Ignore him when the next ladies' choice is announced," Alice proposed. "That way he might take the hint. Ask someone else out."

"I'd like to meet Nick Harris. Maybe I'll ask him. He's on his own and he's great fun."

"Yeah, he's a nice fella," Alice agreed. "He danced with me."

"He was heading towards me once, only that other yoke got there first."

"Give Nick the old glad eye," Margo suggested. "Smile over at him."

"Maybe I will."

"I saw Hacker coming in," Alice informed Margo.

"I copped him," Margo replied. "The pubs must be closed."

"He looked well," Alice said. "He's a fairly good look-ing fella."

"You think so? I see nothing special about him. He's just another Mister Average."

"That friend of his—Toddy, they call him," Eileen smiled. "He's full of himself. I'd say he loves looking at himself in the mirror. He thinks he's God's gift to women."

"Oh God help us," Alice remarked. "And he's useless at dancing—he has two left feet."

Hacker moved forward, deciding he'd ask Margo out to dance.

"And now folks," the band's frontman announced, "the next dance will be a ladies' choice. Come on girls, this is your chance—don't be shy." And then, seemingly out of nowhere, Susie was standing in front of Hacker.

"How about it?" she said. "Are you idle?—that's what some fellows say."

"I'm idle all right." They moved out on the dancefloor. "How are you, Susie?"

"I'm okay. Why did you look away? I thought you were trying to avoid me?"

"No way. Why would I do that?" They danced about slowly to the romantic strains of 'Carolina Moon.' "It's just that I had a couple of girls promised a dance."

"The country one?"

"She's one of them."

"She seems to be fairly popular. You like her?"

"She's a nice girl."

"Nicer than me? Better looking, is she?"

"God no. Sure you're a terrific, gorgeous looking girl. Didn't I always tell you that?"

"I've better legs than her, anyhow—her legs are thick above the ankles."

"Mmmh, I never noticed that."

Susie pressed in against him. A number of couples were dancing close in, with their heads resting on their partners' shoulders. Some of the men had their hands clasped around the girls' lower backs. Margo passed close by, but she averted Hacker's gaze.

"I thought I might have heard from you during the week?" Susie queried.

"I was busy. I had a few things on my mind. I bought a second-hand motor."

"Did you?" Susie said eagerly. "Is it nice? What colour is it?"

"Black—there's only the one colour."

"Is it comfortable? Are the seats comfortable?"

"It's okay—it's nothing to shout home about."

"Will you take me for a spin, Hacker?"

"I will, Susie. As soon as I'm a little better at driving."

"Why? I don't mind. We could pull in someplace nice an' quiet."

"I'd be afraid I might go off the road, hit a ditch and kill you or something. Give me a bit of time."

The three-dance sequence ended and to keep Susie at arm's length Hacker promised they'd dance later. He looked round to see where Margo was standing and positioned himself close by. As soon as "Take your partners for the next dance" rang out, he rushed over and reached Margo first. He was disappointed when a samba was announced. The samba is a particularly energetic form of dance and soon Hacker's shirt felt wet with perspiration. Also, it didn't offer much opportunity for making conversation. The session finished off with the can-can.

"That was tough going," he said. "Margo, would you like a mineral, to cool off?"

"Okay. I'm feeling thirsty, to tell the truth."

They made their way to the mineral bar and located a table near the back. Hacker paid for, and returned with two glasses and a bottle each of orange and lemonade. Margo thanked him. He took out and mopped his brow with a handkerchief.

"God, it's warm tonight," he mumbled.

"You can say that again. I'd say there's thunder around."

"Could be. What do you think of the band—the Dixies?"

"They're good, aren't they?"

"Not as good as the ones last Friday night. They were

125

what you'd call musicians."

"I wasn't here last Friday night."

"That's right. I missed you."

"I'm sure you did. I was far from your mind I'd say."

"No, I'm serious. I look forward to dancing with you—honestly."

"You probably walked Susie Baker home."

"God no, I didn't."

"I saw you before, going off out with her. She has a reputation. Don't you know that?"

"Don't believe all you hear—as far as I can see she's a decent girl."

"She is in my eye! That's not what I heard."

"You heard wrong then. Anyway, I only walked her to her door."

A fellow passing slapped Hacker on the back.

"How yah, Hacker? Hello Margo."

"Hello Pat," they both reply.

"Do you feel the heat? The shirt is stuck to my back."

"That's why we're in here," Hacker responded.

"You know something, Hacker, I'd murder a pint right now."

"You'll have to do with this," Hacker replied, holding up the mineral bottle.

"That's the worst of it." Pat moved on.

"I won't though," Hacker said, taking one of the Baby Powers out of his pocket and pouring it in with the lemonade.

"Jesus, hadn't you enough to drink before you came in?"

"It was late when I got to town. I only had the one bottle."

"I thought I smelt whiskey off your breath. Or maybe you thought the mints might cover it up."

"Margo, listen—I wasn't with Susie Baker last week. Ask anyone."

"Sexy Susie, she's called."

"You're the one I'd really love to be with. You're a lovely, gorgeous looking girl, you know that."

"Oh God! Do you tell that to all the girls? That they're gorgeous?"

"No. Of course I don't."

"Maybe you're one of those old smooth talkers. Are you?"

"A smooth talker," Hacker repeats, grinning.

"An old palaverer?"

"I'm anything but. Instead of that I'm no good at making small talk with girls."

"Go on with you now." She smiled. "I wouldn't believe that"

"You have a lovely smile. Can I ask you something?"

"Go on?"

"Margo, can I give you a lift home?"

"On what?" she smiled again. "On the bar of the bike?"

"On the bar of the bike! We'd look well going along. No, I'm after buying a car—a second-hand one."

"You are! That's nice, that's really nice. It's a surprise. Is it in good nick?"

"It's okay. It's a Ford Prefect."

"I don't know much about them. What colour is it?"

"Black. I'd love to drive you home. Are you on?"

"Listen, I came in with two friends—I wouldn't like to walk out on them. We share the cost. You know the way it is? I'll go for a spin with you some other night—if you like?"

"You will! That's great. Tomorrow night?"

"No, they'd be giving tongue at home if I went out two nights running."

"Sunday night then?"

"Can I trust you, I wonder?"

"Course you can."

"I'm not too sure of you at all, to be honest"

"You can be. Come on, what do you say?"

"Do you know where I live?"

"Your brother told me. Remember when I told you I played football against him? Will I call along?"

"No, I'll be walking down the road."

"They'd be particular about who you went out with? Is that it?"

"No, it's not that. Call along if you like then."

"It's okay—I'll meet you on the road like you said. What time?"

"Let me see." She clicked her fingers. "We finish up around seven, then the supper and getting ready. Say about eight o'clock."

"That's terrific. I'll be looking forward to it. We'll head for the seaside, maybe—if it's a nice evening."

"There was a bus outing to the seaside a few weeks ago. When I was there I went to this fortune teller, and you know what she told me? She said that in the not-too-distant future I was going to meet a tall dark-haired man. You're tall and you're dark-haired."

"I wouldn't mind what she said. She probably tells the same thing to every girl. She was hardly going to tell you that in the not too distant future you were going to meet a randy little leprechaun."

"Oh go on with you!" she smiled again.

A girl at the next table jumped to her feet, in an obvious temper, knocking over a mineral bottle. She stormed out to the dancefloor. Her partner, embarrassed looking, glanced about, hoping no-one he knew witnessed what happened. He then got up and sneaked out to the dancing area also.

"What was that about, I wonder?" Margo commented. "She didn't look too happy."

"You can say that again."

"Listen, Margo, I was going to ask you out before."

"You were?"

"I was afraid you'd say no."

It is announced over the loudspeaker that the next dance will be 'The Siege of Ennis.'

"Come on," Margo said, rising, "we'll dance it."

"Wait'll I finish this."

"Your precious whiskey!"

He tossed back the remainder of his drink and they went out on the floor. Pretty soon the 'The Siege of Ennis' had the Brylcreem and sweat running down the side of Hacker's face. Beads of perspiration stood out on the girls' faces. Margo, laughing, seemed to be enjoying herself hugely, swinging about in gay abandon. Susie Baker glared over at Hacker.

When the session ended, Margo went over to chat with Alice. Hacker went in to the gents' toilet. He contemplated drinking the other Baby Power but decided against it—he might make a fool of himself and say stupid things. He felt pretty pleased with himself that Margo had agreed to meet him. His ego got a big boost. In the back of his mind Susie was still there though. He glanced in the mirror and mopped his face. He'd love to take Susie home when the dance ended. He'd like to try out the back seat of the car. He knew, though, that if Margo heard, then that would be the end of that. Women had a way of getting to know things. Stevie the carpenter came in.

"How's it goin', Hacker?"

"Okay."

"Are you after shiftin'?" Stevie asked, crossing over to the urinal.

"I think so. Yourself?"

"I don't know. I think she's only a teaser. I'll have to wait and see. Heh, did you see what happened to Weird Willie?"

"No, what?"

"He got a few right clatters. You didn't see the commotion?"

"No. I was in the mineral bar."

"You missed it. This big guy overheard a remark Willie passed about his sister. He jumped on him—Christ, he had Willie down on the floor and was batin' the head off him. They had to pull him off him."

"A bit of a batin' wouldn't go astray on Willie."

"You're right there—he's a dangerous whore. I knew that was comin' to him for a good while." They both go back out.

Another Friday night dance drew to a close at The Golden Slipper. Hacker accompanied Margo and Alice down to where the hackney car was parked. Eileen had got her wish as regards Nick Harris; they had gone off to some quiet corner for a cuddle. Hacker had a word with Mossie Dourney about motor cars generally. Eileen, beaming, soon arrived along. As they drove away Hacker waved them all goodbye. One part of him was now telling him to go back to the front area of the dancehall and look for Susie. She didn't appear to have picked up with anyone. The other part was telling him that Margo was too fine and decent a girl to mess up.

He stood back against the wall. Soft rain had begun to fall and he pulled up the collars of his coat. He was glad he didn't have to fall back on the old bike tonight. There was a chip van parked down a piece, at the other side of the dimly lit road. A small queue was starting to form. He contemplated purchasing a bag of their greasy chips. Then he remembered what Toddy had told him: that when the fat guy in the van leant forward drops of sweat fell into the boiling oil. Each time a drop fell in, it made a hissing, sizzling sound.

The wet street looked bleak. He noticed two rats nibbling at a half bag of discarded chips. In the far-off dark distance a dog barked and several others howled a response. He cupped his hands, cracked a match and lit a cigarette. He glanced up and down the road—and then, quickly, back again. There she was, Susie, standing there. She, too, lit up a cigarette and stood back into a doorway.

Game of Chance

Things were not going too smooth in the home of Jimeen Holohan and his wife Minnie. Fights and recurring fights seemed to be the order of the day. Minnie was witnessing all her school friends pushing prams and buggies all over the place. But she had no baby to display to the watching world. This aspect of life would hardly worry some women; it was well known that some women deliberately choose to remain childless. Not Minnie though. She was determined to have a baby no matter what.

The trouble started when Jimeen was picked to play in goal for his local pub in the pubs soccer league. The team was short a player and Jimeen was drafted in to make up the eleven. Now Jimeen never bothered playing sport of any sort. That's why he was placed in goal—the ball might hit off him or something.

In the course of a game against their arch rivals a crucial penalty was awarded to the opposing team. It was up to Jimeen then—to save the penalty and be a hero, or to let in an easy goal and end up the villain. Unfortunately for Jimeen, Samson Fogarty was nominated to be the penalty taker. Now Samson had a kick like the combined total of ten mules. Most of the time his shots flew wide, scorching the grass, or whizzed over the crossbar threatening to go into orbit. But if Samson hit the ball straight then it had the velocity to imperil the safety of even the most experienced of net minders. In this instance he did hit it straight and with a shuddering, sickening impact, Jimeen stopped it with his testicles. He let out a roar that could be heard in the next parish. He was whipped off to hospital in the direst agony.

The unfortunate accident had far reaching consequences. It meant that Jimeen could never again father any offspring. The friction with Minnie started straight away. They went to various doctors in various places but always got the same response—Jimeen's powers of reproduction were damaged irrevocably. He wasn't up to it any more.

Minnie decided that if she couldn't achieve what she wanted with Jimeen she'd get it from someone else. That's when herself and Bud Brady became an item. Jimeen was a bit too naïve and innocent and didn't question why Minnie was so frequently spending nights at her mother's house. The neighbours talked as they always do about such liaisons. Minnie and Bud were seen at various locations: coming out of hotels, walking the beach far from home. Jimeen appeared to be the last to know. That is until someone wrote him an anonymous letter at his place of work, stating: *You stupid idiot. Don't you know Bud Brady is knocking off your wife?*

Jimeen read it and his face turned pale, his knuckles turned white. He asked permission to go home saying he was feeling unwell.

He was working the late shift so his return home would be unexpected. Minnie and Jimeen lived in a cottage up a twisty laneway. Their house, after passing Kirwan's farm, was the last on the road. As Jimeen got near he decided to traverse the final two hundred yards on foot. He switched off the engine and the headlights, parked the car in a gateway and advanced on the house.

As he got near he became aware of a car parked to the rear. As silently as possible he used his key to let himself in. Taking off his shoes he tiptoed down to the bedroom door and listened. The lights were on inside. He heard the bed-springs creaking and low moans.

He threw open the door and burst in, jumping on top of the two on the bed. Bud and Minnie got the shock of their lives. A ferocious fight erupted. Jimeen rained punches at both Bud and Minnie. Jimeen and Bud tumbled out onto the floor where they punched and bit and kicked in a no-quarter-asked-or-given encounter. Minnie ran to the kitchen and came back with the frying-pan. She swung it with force and hit Jimeen on top of the head with the bottom of the pan. He collapsed in a heap.

Some time later he awoke, gingerly feeling the lump on the top of his head. He looked around at the devastation in the room. Practically everything seemed to be knocked over or was in a collapsed state. There was no sign of life so obviously he was on his own. Unsteadily he got to his feet and looked at himself in the mirror. His face was in a bit of a mess. Still, he felt he had given as good as he'd got—if not more. He splashed water on his face and felt better. If nothing else, he felt he had restored his dignity. He explored the rest of the house and noticed some items of value were gone, including the large television. He'd miss the telly.

"The bandy legged whore!" he spat through his teeth.

Also, and more pointedly, all the wedding photos had been removed from the wall, the mantelpiece and the dresser. He sat down by the table and cupped his head in his hands, taking stock of the situation—his wife was gone. That was the stark reality. What a bitch she turned out to be. He again felt his head. His job ran out in a month's time. His cash flow was serious—he owed small amounts of money all over the place. He'd have to cut back on things. The car was due to be taxed.

"Christ above!" He thumped the table with his fist. "She's gone off with that prick. I'll kill the bastard." He'd get himself a cup of tea—at least the electric kettle was still there.

Bud had rented out a small dwelling outside the town. Nobody knew what he did for a living but he always appeared to have plenty of money. Minnie had joined him to unload what they had taken from the house. Bud was feeling very stiff and sore as Jimeen had landed some heavy shots. He had also got a hard kick in the groin which was getting progressively sorer. Could it be that Minnie had landed herself with another dud? Bud struggled with the forty two inch television—Jimeen's pride and joy. Jimeen loved to sit back with a few cans of beer and watch the racing. "It's almost the same as being there," he used to say. Finally, they succeeded in getting the television inside.

"Jesus, I got a terrible shock when the door burst open," Minnie said. "I'm not in the better of it."

"Same here," Bud responded. "My heart nearly stopped—and I do have a little heart murmur, as a matter of fact."

"Do you?"

"Oh, it's nothing. Well," he said, glancing about, "this will be your new home from now on."

"It's fine," Minnie said. She was familiar with the layout in any case. She went down to the bathroom and shouted, "Jesus, I have a black eye!" She quickly came back up. "The little shit hit his own wife."

"Show me. It's not bad."

"Not bad! I'll have to wear dark glasses." Then, in a concerned tone she added, "I wonder did I hurt him bad with the pan?"

"You knocked him out—thank God."

"I hardly killed him, did I?"

"It would take a lot more than that to kill him—he's a tough, wiry kind of guy. I know," he said, feeling his side.

"What a way to end a marriage," Minnie lamented. "The people will talk about us now. We won't be invited to many houses, that's for sure."

"Don't worry. We have each other. Here, we'll have a drink."

"I need something to steady my nerves. Look, my hands are still shaking."

Bud poured out two large vodkas and added a slice of lemon.

"These things blow over," he reassured her. "It's not like the old days."

"When things quieten down we'll have to try and talk to him. Legal things will have to be straightened out."

"In a civilized manner, I hope," Bud said, his hand moving down to the groin area again.

Jimeen and Minnie's split-up soon became common knowledge. Various comments were passed. Some blamed Minnie's fiery temper: "How could any sane man listen to that woman giving tongue day and night." Another said, "She's always complaining. She should learn to wash her dirty clothes in private." Mrs McLoughlan commented, "That one is nothing but a trollop—isn't she after proving it." A few others concluded that Jimeen wasn't blameless: "Sure he spends every penny he earns on booze, horses and that bloody motor car. Hard for her to put up with it." Another said, "He's a madman driving—the speed he tears around the roads in—mark my words, he'll be killed yet. I hate saying it, but it looks that way."

Minnie finally hung Jimeen out to dry when she confided to Roy Lacey's wife Jackie that Jimeen was useless in bed ever since Samson shattered his testicles with the football. This gave rise to a lot of merriment amongst Jimeen's peers. Perhaps black humour might be a better description.

Jimeen found the going tough on his own. He was fond of company and found the solitude he was now experiencing a wee bit disconcerting, to say the least. His job at the factory was demanding and he found he needed regular sleep. "That bloody job will be gone too," he moaned. "What will I do then?" Work was getting harder and harder to find. The bills were starting to mount up. He toyed with the idea of emigrating to Australia. He was a bad cook. He was living on boiled eggs, tea and bread. There were egg-shells all over the place.

Wednesday turned out to be a particularly bad day: when he got home from work he found the house had been ransacked. It must have been Minnie and Bud, he concluded—knowing he was away at work they called and stripped the place. Nothing was left but the bare essentials. He decided he'd buy an Alsatian—a ferocious dog who'd tear strips off anyone who crossed the threshold.

Down at Kirwan's farm, Dickie, Samson and Harry Kirwan were standing over a large modern rotovator. There was something wrong with the machine and they couldn't figure out what the problem was. Samson, the tractor driver, said he noticed a rattling sound first and then a loud screeching noise. He thought at first it might free itself, but then decided it was wiser to take it home to the yard.

"You took a chance travelling the road with that thing behind you," Harry said. "You took a big risk."

"I suppose I did," Samson replied.

"Look at the width of it. You had right to use your mobile."

"To tell the truth it never entered my head," Samson admitted.

"Sure there's no traffic on that road," Dickie ventured.

"Jimeen is on it," Harry reminded him. "And he travels that road the same as if it was Brand's Hatch or Silverstone. In all seriousness you'd want flashing lights ahead and behind with that machine."

"Christ I can't see anything," Samson mumbled from underneath. He stood up wiping his oil-stained hands on a piece of cloth. "We'll have it taken asunder the way we're going."

"I can't get this feckin' nut loose," Dickie grumbled, straining himself.

"Show me," Samson said. Using his strong arms he prised the nut loose with little or no effort.

"I was afraid it would shear," Dickie remarked.

"It was in there somewhere," Samson now pointed. "It sounded like steel rubbing on steel."

"And the forecast is bad for tomorrow evening," Dickie informed Harry.

"You always have the bad word, you know that" Harry shot back, adding, "You're worse than the blight."

"The long range forecast is bad. I'm just telling you."

"I know it is. But them fellas in the Met can be wrong too."

"Could a stone be caught somewhere? Often times it's a silly thing," Samson suggested.

"I know," Harry agreed, "but still you can't take a chance. That bloody machine cost a fair penny. Christ, the price of everything is gone up in the moon."

"I hear the price of diesel is going up again," Dickie now tells Harry."

"Did you ever hear anything good, did you?"

"Maybe if I kept going it might have freed itself."

"God no, don't ever do that—it would be too chancy," Harry advised him. "This kind of thing now would get under your skin. Look," he pulls on a belt, "everything seems free enough."

Breda, Harry's wife, appears and calls, "Come on in for a bit of supper. It's ready."

"Come on, I'm hungry," Harry said. "We'll come back to it with fresher minds."

Jimeen was taking the top off his second boiled egg. Earlier he had noticed red spots breaking out on his legs and upper arms. *It could be too many eggs*, he surmised. Maybe he'd better start striking into town for some takeaways. He looked around at his miserable surroundings. He thought he heard a mouse scratching.

He suddenly remembered that this was Wednesday evening—Lotto night. Minnie was the one who usually bought the tickets. For the main prize they always did the same numbers: 10, 12, 17, 23, 30, and 36, with 37 as the bonus number.

He glanced at his watch and realized he'd better get a move on. How many times did they mark down those numbers? Jimeen was afraid that he might forget some night, and that's the very night the bloody numbers might come up. What would he do then? *Jump in the river.*

He decided he'd call to White's pub for a pint or two on the way back. He quickly changed out of his working clothes, had a quick wash, put on a clean shirt, jeans and jacket, grabbed his wallet and headed out to the car. He didn't even bother locking the door—he had no reason to now. *Whatever else,* he thought, as he started up the car, *I'll have to buy a television.* He missed the racing and the football. *Them other two whores-ghosts are probably sitting on their fat arses right now, watching fuckin' Coronation Street on my forty-two inch.*

He moved onto the road. Then he thought, *What if my numbers came up? She'd be demanding half the money. Christ, I never thought of that. She always threw in twenty euro at the start of every month. Even if I denied it she could still make big trouble. There could even be court cases. Feck it, I'll change a couple of numbers. I'll change the twelve to thirteen and the thirty to thirty-one. From now on I'll be living a new lifestyle, so I might as well have new numbers. It's all a waste of money anyhow. I'm nothing but an idiot.*

He revved up the car. He loved driving. The car, which he kept spotless, was his pride and joy.

Harry, Samson and Dickie came out from their supper and were recommencing work on the rotovator. They heard the roar of the car coming down the road and Jimeen whizzed past the gate.

"Christ, he's some madman," Harry commented.

"There's no sense to that," Dickie said, shaking his head. "If a child stepped out on the road he couldn't stop."

"I'm afraid something will stop him one of those days," Harry added. "He'll come to grief I'm afraid. That's the sad part of it."

"Remember the evening of the match—the penalty?" Dickie said to Samson. "I think you gelded him, you know that."

"Don't be reminding me of it." Samson said, worried looking. Samson was a big, soft guy, who would hate to injure anyone.

"That's what I heard," Dickie continued.

"Don't believe everything you hear," Harry remarked.

"That's the reason Minnie left him. Jimeen can't produce the goods anymore."

"Idle gossip—and gossip can be a dangerous thing," Harry commented."

"Did you see the way he stood in the goal that evening?" Dickie grinned, "With his two hands out like *that*, like a scarecrow. And the roars out of him when the ball connected. We all nearly fell down laughing." He laughs again.

"If you were on the receiving end of it you wouldn't laugh," Harry reminded him.

"You have a kick like a mule, Samson, you know that. That ball was travelling like a Scud missile."

"I was never so sorry about anything in my life," Samson sighed. "That's as true as I'm standing here. I keep thinking of it."

"Ah, sure it was an accident," Dickie consoled him.

"Put your minds to what we're at here and don't mind your penalty kicks. I have to go out later on or she'll lose the head. We have arranged to meet a couple in town."

Harry, Dickie and Samson grew up together in the same townsland. Dickie and Samson worked for Harry, but apart from that they were also friends. They often stayed on after hours, free of charge, to help Harry repair machinery. They enjoyed that type of work and the banter that went with it. On midweek evenings Dickie and Samson had nothing much better to do.

Jimeen went into the shop and purchased his National Lottery ticket.

"It's a big one tonight," Mr. Finch, the shopkeeper, informed him, as if he didn't know already.

"It would be worth winning tonight all right," Jimeen responded.

"What would you do if your numbers came up?" Mr. Finch asked as he counted out the change.

"I often heard people ask that," Jimeen said. What would I do?" He scratched his head. "I'd go to Thailand where all the sexy women are and spend the rest of my life there."

"Would you?" Mr. Finch repeated eagerly, giving off the distinct impression that he would like to do exactly the same himself.

"I might as well now, seeing that the squaw is after leaving me. Did you know that?"

"No."

"That's a wonder. Everybody else seems to know. They keep reminding me anyhow."

"Don't worry, Jimeen—you're not the only one."

"She went off with that basterin' Bud Brady. He's a bad whore, that fella."

"Is he?"

"I'm telling you, you couldn't meet worse. If he comes in here don't leave him out of your sight. I heard he'd rob the cross off an ass's back."

"That so?"

What Jimeen said wasn't actually the truth, but then all's fair in love and war.

"I gave him a hiding though," he next told Mr. Finch. "A real hiding."

"Good man."

"The bandy-legged bastard! I'll give you one bit of good advice, Mr. Finch—beware of a bandy-legged man. He's over-sexed, for one thing."

"What about a bandy-legged woman?" Mr. Finch, queried eagerly.

"The very same—even worse."

"Bandy-legged women are fond of it then?" Mr. Finch concluded, eyes agape.

"They can't get enough of it."

"Can't they?"

It was widely rumoured that Mrs. Finch never let Mr. Finch near her sexually. She felt it was all dirty. That could explain why Mr. Finch had such an inordinate interest in all things sexual.

"I'll be off then," Jimeen said, as another customer came up to the counter.

"No, hold on…"

But Jimeen was gone. He went out, jumped into the car and headed for White's pub. Bud, he felt, wouldn't be welcome the next time he called on Mr. Finch. He swung in to the car park behind the pub, sending pebbles flying.

When he entered there was no greeting from the others as they were all too familiar with each other to bother.

"A pint of Heineken, is it?" Alfie the publican asked from habit.

"Yeah, a Heineken," Jimeen replied, taking the money from his pocket. Roy, Denny and Jerry, three young men, were in conversation close by.

"How are things Jimeen?" Jerry asked.

"Not too bad," Jimeen responded.

"Could be better, I'd say," Roy remarked with a grin.

Jimeen never liked Roy. The ignorant pig was always giving digs.

"Did the woman come back yet?" Denny asked.

"No, nor she won't, so don't be fuckin' asking me about her."

"You're not alone. People are breaking up all over the place," Jerry said, holding out his fingers. "I could name several from round here."

"Still, it's hard coming home to a lonely house," Roy said.

"It grows on you, you know that?" Jimeen responded. "I'm starting to enjoy it."

"That's the ticket," Alfie said.

"No one to rear up on you," Jimeen continued. "You couldn't please the bitch I was saddled with."

"I always thought Minnie was a nice girl," Roy commented.

"You should try living with her then. A bit of peace in the head is what I want now."

"We all want that," Alfie agreed, "and in this business it's a hard thing to find."

"She's after shackin' up with Bud Brady," Jerry announced. "He's a bit of a quare hawk."

"He's a bit of a mystery man," Roy added. "Where's he getting the money from? The son-of-a-bitch didn't do a day's work since he came back from England. He plays golf. He's laughing at us all boy—laughing at the fools."

"Living off the state again," Denny said bitterly. "We're working and paying taxes to keep bastards like him in luxury."

"The bandy-legged whore!" Jimeen repeated with venom.

"How's the country able to keep going at all?" Jerry asked, with a hint of irony. "The working man is being screwed the whole time. Bud and his likes could be drawing free money in several places. I don't know, there's something wrong somewhere."

"You know something else," Roy said, "if you brought in a dozen German businessmen they'd do a better job at running the bloody country than that shower of gobshites up there in the Dail. Do you know that?"

"You mightn't be too far wrong at all," Alfie agreed.

"It's the truth," Roy emphasized. "They're all the same—useless…"

"Anyway, you know what we were discussing, Jimeen, before you came in—we were debating about who was the best player Alex Ferguson bought since he took over at Manchester United? Who would you say now? You're well up on those things."

"There were a few. Straight away, Eric Cantona springs to mind."

"He'd be my choice," Roy agreed.

"Then you have Keane, Giggs, Ferdinand," Jimeen continued. "Ronaldo would be up there."

"What about Rooney?" Gerry queried.

"God, you're right, Rooney is a right one. Still, in my opinion Peter Schmeichel was the best player Ferguson ever bought."

"That's what I said," Alfie declared. "Good man, Jimeen."

"One goalkeeper would say that about another, wouldn't he?" Roy grinned. "Jimeen, do you know the difference between Peter Schmeichel and you?"

Jimeen braced himself for some smart-assed comment, and he wasn't disappointed.

"Schmeichel stopped the ball with his hands."

All laughed at this remark except Jimeen.

"Sssh," Alfie said, "they're giving out the Lotto numbers. Where'll I get a piece of paper?" He rummaged.

The announcer called out the Lotto Plus and the Lotto Plus Two first. Then she announced: "Now we have the main prize for tonight which is a whopping three million, two hundred thousand, three hundred and seventy-two euro. And good luck to you all. Here now are the numbers drawn… the first one out is number ten, uimhir deich… the second out is number thirteen, thirteen lion… the third number out is number seventeen, seacht lion."

"I have three anyhow," Jimeen said to himself.

"The fourth lucky number is number twenty-three, uimhir twenty tri,"

"I have four." He was getting excited now.

"… and now the fifth one out is number thirty one, uimhir thirty aon"

"Jesus, keep going, keep going!"

"… and the final number for this evening is number thirty-six, uimhir trioca se."

"I have them!" Jimeen said to himself in awe. "I have them."

He hardly heard the announcer saying, "And the bonus number is forty-one, agus ta an lion bonus forty aon."

Jimeen felt the blood drain from his face. He'd won the Lotto! His hands started to tremble. He looked around him. Everything appeared normal. "Stay calm, Jimeen," he said to himself, "Stay calm." He felt his heart thumping. His normal heartbeat was around sixty-five to the minute. It must be doing one hundred and thirty now, he felt.

"People will be asking me did I get the numbers," Alfie said.

In a daze, Jimeen stared straight ahead.

"Are you all right there, Jimeen?" Alfie asked

"Yeah… just thinkin'…"

"Oh aye. But sure things might sort themselves out yet."

"I'm going to give up spending money on this bloody Lotto," Denny said, crunching his worthless ticket.

Control yourself, Jimeen's inner voice said. He looked at himself in the mirror facing him from behind the bar. Everything seemed normal all right, but it would never be normal again. He found it hard to control the tremor in his hands. He gripped the pint glass tight.

"I'll have you in a game of darts," Roy said to Denny. "For five euro."

"You're on. Make it ten, okay?"

"Right, come on. The best of three."

Jerry opened out the Evening Herald and started to read.

Jimeen vaguely heard Roy repeat to Denny, "Schmichel stopped the ball with his hands. That was a good one, wasn't it?" He laughed again at his own joke.

Jerry leant over and whispered to Jimeen, "Don't mind that feckin' Roy—he's only a bollox."

Jimeen nodded his head.

Roy started to sing as he lined up the darts:

> *Hitler had only one big ball,*
> *Goering had two but they were small,*
> *Himmler had something similar,*
> *but Goebbels had no balls at all.*

Previously that would have provoked a reaction, but not this time. Jimeen was finding the euphoria overpowering.

Back at Kirwan's farm the problem with the rotovator had been solved. Harry had taken his wife out as planned.

Samson had volunteered to work late into the night seeing how the forecast was so bad for the following evening.

"Good. Thanks, Samson," Harry had said, "we'll get a good bit done tomorrow then, before the rain."

Dickie's mobile phone had rung and he had moved to one-side and held a short, muffled conversation. Samson put the cap back on the tank of the tractor, after filling up with diesel.

"You go on ahead of me with the car then," he said to Dickie.

"Be Christ I won't."

"What?"

"That was the bird ringing—she's stuck for a lift in town. There was some kind of mix-up."

"What am I going to do so?" Samson asked.

"Put a red rag on the outside."

"What good would a red rag be in the dark?"

"Ah, there'll be no-one on that road. Flash your lights if you see Jimeen coming. I'm off, good-luck."

Samson pondered the situation for a minute. Then he moved the powerful machinery out on to the road, the rotovator overlapping the tractor by a few feet.

At that moment Jimeen, struggling hard to contain his emotions, got down off the barstool. He'd go home and think things over, try and get his head straight. He'd make a phone call, to be certain. It felt like it, but could he have peed some in his pants?

"Good-luck," He mumbled to Jerry.

"Be seeing you," Jerry said, without taking his eyes off the paper.

Alfie was busy stacking the shelves, and didn't see him leave.

"So-long, Schmeichel," Roy said. Jimeen ignored him.

He jumped in behind the wheel and revved up the engine as he had the habit of doing. As he drove away he shouted "Yipee!" and clenched his fist above his head. *Thank You God, for having pity on me! Thank You. I must give a good sum to charity. No-one must know yet! Definitely no-one must know. My mother and father will be taken care of, and my sister Jane. Feck the rest of 'em. All they ever did was make fun of me.* The adrenalin was pumping through him at the enormity of what he had won. *I'm a millionaire. Me! A millionaire!*

He rounded a bend and saw lights flashing in front him. Loose battery leads, he presumed. At the last second he spotted the rotovator. Slamming the brakes he yanked the steering to the left and scraped along the side of the fence—the car hopped a couple of times, almost turning over. His head hit the door. At least he'd made it—he had avoided the deadly machine. He got out, put his hand to his head, felt a bit unsteady on his feet. Samson had jumped down off the tractor.

"Oh Christ Jimeen, I'm sorry, I'm sorry. Are you all right?

"Are you trying to kill me, Samson? Jesus, bringing that out on the road, with no-one in front or behind."

"I know. I'm sorry, I'm awful sorry. Are you all right though?"

"I don't know what way I am. I could have been killed."

"Did you hit your head?"

"Off the door. It's okay, I'm okay."

"Are you sure?" Samson said, studying Jimeen.

"I could be in bits. You could be ringing for an ambulance right now. You know that?"

"I know I could. What kind of idiot am I? Is the car badly damaged?" They both look at the large indent up the left-hand side. "The insurance will cover all that. I'll admit full responsibility. Christ, Jimeen, you don't know how sorry I am. I got some fright when I saw you coming."

"Not half as big as the one I got when I spotted that."

"You're not hurt bad, anyhow. That's all that matters. You did great driving, the way you squeezed through." He noticed Jimeen feeling his head. "Maybe it would be safer to see a doctor?"

"Samson, I'm okay. I have to go now. I'm in an awful hurry."

"No, hold on. Christ hold on. Are you all right to drive? The steering could be damaged."

"I'll tell you what way it is tomorrow."

"Harry and myself will call up early. Will you be there?"

"Maybe."

Samson is examining the car again. "You'll need two new doors, and a new panel, I'd say. Jimeen, don't worry about money now, or anything like that. Everything will be fixed as good as new. You're probably like myself, and don't have a bob to spare."

"That's right, not a fluke. Samson I'm in a mad hurry. Good-luck."

Jimeen got back into the car and drove away. It was pulling a bit to one-side. His ankle was starting to feel sore. *I must have caught it in the pedals. The thick idiot, out on the road with that machine. I could have been killed or badly injured. In a wheelchair, maybe, and the ticket in my pocket.* Despite everything, Jimeen had good time for Samson. *I'll have to slow down in future. That was a warning. I don't want anything to happen to me now—not with this.* He pats his breast pocket. *What could have happened though—a millionaire one minute and dead the next. Oh God, thank You a second time. A millionaire! I wonder was I the only winner?* The aftershock of the accident started to recede. The euphoria, exhilaration and excitement returned. He again felt on top of the world. *I'll disguise myself when I go to Dublin to collect the money.*

As Jimeen drove along his mind was cluttered with all kinds of thoughts about what he was going to do. And then he saw it, parked beside the house: the same car as before—Bud's car. He pulled over, turned off the headlights. He'd give himself a minute to sort his wits. "Christ, what do they want this time? Something important or they wouldn't be here. Something to do with the house, maybe. They're up to no good, anyhow. He might be better off to turn round and keep going."

Curiosity got the better of him—he'd go in. He felt his temper surfacing again, but knew on this occasion he'd have to control it. His inner voice said, *You pulled it off in the pub, so play it cool, Jimeen, play it ice cool. After all, only for Bud you wouldn't have changed the numbers. You'd have had four and won about forty euro. Good man, Bud, for your choice in women!* He realized also that the affection he once had for Minnie had evaporated, was gone for ever. What did he care about Bud and Minnie now? He'd drive up, walk in and confront them. He'd confuse them by acting as if the whole situation was completely normal. He turned the lights back on, drove up and parked behind Bud's car.

He opened the door, entered, and there they were: Minnie wearing that awful blue track-suit that Jimeen despised, with the perpetual fag dangling out of her gob It's a wonder, he thought, she wasn't wearing the filthy pyjamas she often wore, even when going to the shops.

152

And Bud, standing back, wearing his dark glasses, with a baseball bat clutched in his hands in a threatening manner.

"Take it easy now, Jimeen," Bud said. "Try something funny and I'll use this. I mean it."

"What do you two want? Make it quick, I'm in a hurry. You want the last of the furniture, is that it? The old table there?"

"I paid for nearly all that furniture when I was working," Minnie informed him.

"You paid for half of it."

Jimeen went across, rolled back the corner of the faded carpet, put his hand in and took out two hundred euro he had hidden there for the rainy day. "We had four numbers in the lotto draw."

"I noticed that," Minnie replied."

"Here," he said, "you might as well have half—for old time's sake." He flicked a twenty euro note across to her, which fell to the floor. "We used to share our good luck, Bud."

Minnie bent down to pick up the money, saying, "What about my share of the house? Half of it is mine. That's why we're here."

"That's the law," Bud reminded him.

"Not when she walks off with some bandy-legged tramp."

"That's where you're mistaken, mate," Bud contradicted him. Bud was actually afraid of Jimeen and held the baseball bat in a defensive mode.

"We'll have to get a solicitor," Minnie said.

"Oh do. Get your solicitor, by all means," Jimeen replied. "Bud, are you enjoying watching my forty two inch television?" Jimeen asked with cynicism. "It's almost the same as being there, isn't it?"

"We know you like watching the racing and the football so we brought you one," Minnie said.

"Oh did you now. That's very kind of you. Is this it here?"

There was a cardboard box on the table. Jimeen opened it and took out a small, used, fourteen inch Grundy television. He lifted it over his head and sent it crashing into the fireplace. Glass and a multiple of other bits flew all over the floor. Bud gave a little jump backwards on his bow legs, holding the baseball bat like a Samurai sword.

Minnie got a shock. "What are you doing? Christ above!"

"There's no need for that!" Bud said "Careful now," he warned.

Jimeen smiled demurely, looked from one to the other. Minnie wondered did he miss her so much he was going queer in the head.

"I'm off now," Jimeen said, still smiling.

"No, wait, we have a lot to discuss. No use putting things on the long finger," Minnie pointed out.

"Can't we talk about things in a civilized fashion. There was no need for that," Bud said, pointing to the floor.

"No more talk," Jimeen said, putting his finger to his lips. "We're done talking. White man speak with forked tongue. I'm off then."

"What are you rushing for? Where are you going?"

Jimeen pointed to the window. "Minnie, there's a whole big wide world out there. That's where I'm going."

"When are we going to talk then?" Minnie asked again.

"That's in the lap of the gods, I'd say." He stood at the

door and with a flourish of the hand said, "If you want to spend the night here, you're welcome. Be my guests." He departed.

Bud and Minnie looked at each other. "What do you make of that?" Minnie asked

"That man is nuts. He's a blackguard too—look what he done with the telly. I told you you'd get no satisfaction from that lunatic."

"He'd put your heart crossways. And the feckin' money hid under the carpet. You'd never think of looking there, sure you wouldn't?"

A car was heard to start up and drive away.

"There he's off," Minnie said bitterly.

"Good riddance," Bud added. "I'd say he'll do his best now to make things difficult for us."

"Did you see the head on him—grinning from ear to ear. He's off on a skite now, with that money from under the carpet. That and the miserable twenty he won on the lotto. Holy Jesus up in Heaven, you'd think he had won the whole feckin' lot."

Confrontation

Betty and Dave are enjoying a cup of coffee and cake at Julie's, their favourite café, overlooking Wexford Harbour. Prints of sailing ships on the walls give the location an air of authenticity. Julie's is renowned for its confectionery and the pleasant service provided. Two pretty, smiling girls are on hand as assistants to Julia, the proprietress. If business is slack, Julie likes nothing better than to sit down and have a chat with her customers. In this capacity, she is sitting at the table with Betty and Dave.

Julia comments that mid-week is always a bit on the quiet side.

"It wasn't too quiet around lunchtime," Betty remarks, "We passed along here and the place was packed."

"Don't get me wrong, I'm not complaining. People like to chat, with a cup of tea or coffee."

"It's the quality on offer," Betty smiles, flattering.

"The two girls there are great," Julie confirms. "But I'll tell you one thing, this recession is hitting the town hard. I went for a good long walk yesterday evening and I couldn't believe it, girl, all the places that are closed down."

"It's a bloody disgrace," Dave agrees.

"Old established places," Julia continues, "that were there for generations, gone. I hate to see the old names disappearing—the traditional names. The town will never be the same again."

"The heart and soul is being torn out of the small town centres by those big multinationals on the outskirts," Dave declares.

"Oh I'd say you're right," Julie nods. "The sad fact is the small shops just can't compete."

"It's the same everywhere," Betty points out. "I could name several towns."

"And to think a couple of years ago everywhere was booming," Julie laments. "The Celtic Tiger built us all up to drop us back down with a bang."

"You know who's to blame for that?" Dave says.

"Sure the dogs in the street know who's to blame," Julie replies. "And they'll get away with it—don't they always?"

"If this was America they'd be arrested," Betty emphasises.

"If this was China they'd probably be shot." Dave adds.

"No rest for the wicked," Julie says, rising, as four young girls enter. The four girls order coffee and pick out their confectionery of choice from behind the glass display cabinet. They then go and sit by a table near the window, talking in the animated, excited fashion, that young people are prone to do.

"Do you fancy anything else?" Dave asks Betty.

"God, no. All those calories. I'm too fat as I am."

"No you're not—you're just right. I don't like girls who are too skinny—like Beckham's wife."

"Victoria. All the top models nowadays are skinny."

"They look unhealthy to me. Anyway, men don't like walking skeletons. They like something warm and soft to hold on to."

"Skinny is the way the top fashion designers want them."

"That's because most of the top fashion designers are gay. They don't appreciate sexy, curvy women."

"Maybe there's a happy medium somewhere."

"Maybe. What the hell about it. Will we head for the sea then? Isn't that what you had in mind?"

"We have nothing else to do around town? Sure we haven't?"

Dave shrugs his shoulders, "I don't think so."

They stand up, look to say goodbye to Julie but she has gone into the kitchen. They have parked the car in the church car-park and make their way in that direction.

"It's a great day to be doing nothing," Dave says, as they meander along. He starts to sing in a low, unobtrusive voice:

> *Up in the morning out on my job work like a devil*
> *for my pay,*
> *But that lucky old sun has nothing to do but roll*
> *around heaven all day.*

"There's a nice dress," Betty remarks as they pass a ladies' boutique.

"A nice price too."

"It's not too bad. The prices have come down. You mightn't agree with me, but they have. Lots of things have come down."

Dave points to a fuel display sign. "Petrol is not one of them."

They link arms as they stroll along. Betty is an attractive, tall brunette, aged twenty-six, neatly dressed in appropriate, simple clothes for a day at the beach. Dave is of average build, with dark hair, slim, wearing Wranglers, denim jacket, wine coloured shirt. Both work in the catering industry. Due to a hectic weekend schedule they've been rewarded with an extra free day.

"Left or right?" Dave queries. "Rosslare or Curracloe?"

"Curracloe," Betty decides.

Having reached Dave's car they get in and drive down Wexford's narrow streets, across the long bridge that straddles the harbour estuary, and on out the Gorey-Dublin road. They drive for around six kilometres, slow down and turn right for their destination. They pass the little hamlet of Curracloe and follow the signs pointing to the beach. Curracloe is a quiet, pleasant, unspoiled area. The approach road leads in to the large car-park from where the sea is not yet visible—a high, wide embankment of sand separates the sea from the land. (A good proportion of the east coast of Ireland has a sandbank as a defence against the encroaching tide.) Adjacent to the car-park there is an arcade with indoor games and fast food. On quiet days—as on this occasion—it remains closed. Wooden walkways ascend and descend on to the beach. The beach itself is vast and attractive with packed, fine sand, making it ideal for walking. It appears to stretch up the coast for miles. Curracloe was the beach used for the famous D-Day Landing battle scenes in the film *Saving Private Ryan*.

Having parked the car, Betty takes out the beach-bag containing their swim gear and they amble out on to the beach. They move to the water's edge and back, and locate a nice spot for a bit of sunbathing. The day is sunny and pleasant, ideal for the seaside. It being mid-week and early in the season, they appear to have the place entirely to themselves.

"God, that beach stretches for miles," Dave observes.

"Yeah, if you were super-fit you could walk to Dublin."

160

They spread out the beach towels and dress down to their swimming outfits. Betty's consists of a revealing, skimpy two-piece.

"I'm going in for a dip," Dave announces. "You're not, I'd say? I need hardly ask?"

"No, the water's too cold yet. It's still only early May you know."

"Coward," Dave jokes, as he heads out. 'She was right—it's fairly cold all right,' he acknowledges to himself. "But only for the first few seconds" he says aloud, as he plunges into an oncoming wave. The initial shock over, his body adjusts to the temperature. He now embraces the crisp pleasure of sea and sun.

Betty raises her head, observing Dave swimming and frolicking in the water. She's aware that this is going to be her first full day alone with Dave. So far it has gone okay. But then a day is nothing—it's only a day. A friend once told her that it was hugely important to spend as much time as possible alone with someone if you really wanted to know what that person was like. She, herself, had known several couples who had gone away on holidays together and it signalled the end of their affairs. Over the two weeks together they sadly discovered that it would never work out between them—they were just incompatible. After about twenty minutes Dave returns and dries himself down with a towel from the bag.

"Was that nice?" Betty asks him.

"Great," he replies. "There's something about the sea—the salt water on your lips and the waves crashing. There's a theory, isn't there, that we originated from the sea?"

"So going in for a swim then is a bit like going home," Betty smiles.

"Exactly," Dave replies as he stretches down beside her. He admires the contours of her body. "You have a great body, you know that?"

"No, I have not. I'm too fat."

"Don't be ridiculous."

Betty requests, and he rubs suncream on her shoulders and back. She does the same to him. Both lie back.

"This is the life," Dave says contentedly.

"The sound of the sea is soothing," Betty responds.

Dave leans over, kissing her on the cheek. "We'll just close our eyes and relax then." They savour the peace and quiet.

Some young local, teenage boys arrive along and start kicking a plastic beach-ball about. Dave becomes aware that the ball is kicked in their direction far more often than one might expect. Then a thirteen or fourteen year old would slouch over and take his time retrieving the ball. It struck Dave that the ball was used as a ploy by those testosterone-driven youths to get a close-up of Betty's semi-naked body.

He mentions it to her and she smiles, saying, "You're joking!"

"Watch then," Dave says. The ball duly sails over.

"We'll go," Betty quickly decides. She stands up and blanketing herself with the beach towel she dresses. Dave does likewise.

"Little feckers, aren't they?" she says. "What'll they be like when they're bigger?"

"I should grab that ball and launch it with an almighty kick out towards the sea."

"Don't, you'd only draw their ire down on us. Oh, what about it!"

"Will we go for a good walk along the beach? We'll

162

find someplace a bit more private."

"Okay."

"I don't know about you," Dave says, "but whether it was the swim or the sea breeze, but I feel like a sandwich."

"We're not long out of Julie's!"

"I know."

They return to the car and deposit the damp towel and swimsuit in the boot. Dave takes out the picnic basket they have brought along and treats himself to a cup of tea and a couple of sandwiches. Betty says she'll wait till later. After being to the toilet nearby, Betty looks around, observing the overgrown, desolate area behind the dunes running parallel to the beach, and the pathway or narrow roadway running through it.

Dave suggests they take the beach towels and Betty packs them into a shoulder bag. They set off at a brisk pace and laugh as each tries to out-walk the other. After a while the pace slows to a leisurely stroll. Looking about, and noticing they are unobserved, they entwine arms and kiss.

"Ever notice," Dave says, "that you rarely get tired walking on a beach? Is it because it's so flat, I wonder?"

"I like walking barefoot, feeling the sand between my toes."

They suddenly observe two figures, two men, idling near the dunes. They are drinking cans of beer and smoking cigarettes. One is bearded. They turn away as Dave and Betty approach. Betty throws them a cursory glance, Dave takes little notice. After another ten minutes or so they halt. Dave looks back.

"We've come a good bit," he indicates. "We might find a comfortable spot up there."

They move about and locate a cosy sun-trap of a soft

space, between two sand dunes. They again spread out the beach towels.

"I hope there are no creepy-crawlies here," Betty says.

"I didn't see any snakes or lizards on the way down—there might be a few crocodiles in that marshy spot over there."

"*Jurassic Park!*"

They lower themselves down on the towels, feeling the hot sand beneath. The suncream is again produced and liberally applied to faces, necks and arms. They lie close together, Betty's head resting on Dave's shoulder.

"Working a fourteen hour day can get to you. I'm feeling tired today," Betty admits. "Are you?"

"I'm not too bad. But then, I don't cover as much ground as you. That's why you look so fit, so well—so beautiful."

"Don't be joking me," Betty retorts with a smile, "I'm not beautiful—far from it."

"You are."

"I read in a magazine recently that a large proportion of girls hate certain parts of their own appearance. Would you believe that?"

"It's hard to credit it," Dave responds, shrugging shoulders. "but then, you hear so many queer things that nothing is inclined to surprise you anymore."

"They get depressed," the article said. "When they look in the mirror they despise themselves. Imagine that."

"It must be some form of mental thing," Dave suggests. "Is it?"

"Maybe. Or maybe it's the pressure coming at girls from every angle. All the images of those glamorous models staring out at you from everywhere. 'You, too, must have a figure like this.'

"The Victoria type?"

"Yes. Then when the average plain Jane looks at her reflection in the mirror it's no wonder she feels depressed. She then starts out on a diet she can't keep. That makes her feel even worse. The next step is liposuction, or some form of plastic surgery."

"One thing for sure, you'll never have to go down that route."

"I don't know. I'm not too fond of what I see in the mirror either."

"That's rubbish talk."

"I'll be going to no doctor, anyhow. So don't worry."

"Good. Some men go for special treatments too, don't they?"

"They go to get a certain part enlarged." Both laugh over this.

"I don't know what my poor old granny would make of it at all," Dave says.

"The world is changing so fast I wonder what will it be like in fifty years time?"

"The world's population will have increased by so much that Ireland will be overrun. Hunger will drive people here from all over Africa."

"Who knows? We'll still be around by then—hopefully."

"The average lifespan will be close to a hundred," Dave surmises.

"A hundred! I don't know would I like to live to be that age."

"But I prefer the here and now," Dave declares, planting a light kiss on Betty's lips. "Lying here on the warm sand with the girl of my dreams—what more could a man ask for?"

"I'm always afraid of being over-optimistic about anything, you know that. A little nagging voice in the back of my head keeps telling me, 'You'll pay for this yet.' That's being stupid, I suppose?"

"I never felt more optimistic than I do now. You make me feel that way."

"That's good. This is a relaxing spot. We're all alone—a million miles from the hustle and bustle of hotel life." After a moment, Betty raises herself up on her elbows and looks out towards the sea. "Sea and sand, everywhere," she vaguely whispers."

"What?"

"Imagine being shipwrecked and ending up on a desert island—nothing to look at every day but sea and sand."

"Like old Robinson Crusoe."

"I heard a joke along those lines the other day. It's a bit funny, but not terribly funny—do you want to hear it, anyway?"

"Why not?"

"These three fellows were ship-wrecked and ended up on a desert island. They were walking along the beach one day when they came across this peculiar shaped bottle. They uncorked the bottle and up rose a genie."

"The old genie one again," Dave grins.

"Yes. In thanks for being freed from the bottle the genie granted each one a single wish. The first fellow, a Scotsman, said he'd like to be back home with his family and friends again. Then whoosh! He suddenly found himself back in Aberdeen. The second fella, an Englishman, said he'd like the same. In a flash he was transported back to Somerset. The third fellow, a Wexford man—"

"Hold on," Dave interrupts, "a Wexford man! He

wasn't a Kilkenny man, or a Carlow man, by any chance?"

"No," Betty giggles, "he was a Wexford man. The genie, with a big toothy smile then asked, 'And now Master, what is your wish?' The Wexford man scratched his head and said, 'I'm starting to feel a bit lonely now—I'd like to have my two friends back again.'"

Both laugh a little.

"You could call that going nowhere fast."

"Or," Betty adds, "come back, all is forgiven." Betty suddenly tenses up, becoming alert. "Dave," she says, with a distinct note of urgency which causes him to sit up. "Look over there. No, keep down!"

They observe two hooded men slinking along between the sand dunes as if searching. As they round a knoll the pair become more visible.

"Aren't those the two we saw on the beach?" Betty now asks with trepidation.

"The two on the beach had no hoods."

"They had something draped on their arms. One of them had a beard too." She becomes alarmed. "Those are the same two. There was no-one else."

"What are they looking for?" Dave asks with growing concern.

"Could be us," Betty retorts. "I heard of a couple who were attacked."

"Attacked!"

"Come on, quick! I don't like the look of them," Betty urges.

"Me neither. Christ! We'll move, come on, come on"

"Leave the towels—keep down," Betty commands.

"We'll get on the pathway—we'd be able to move quicker—keep low." Dave stresses.

They move out onto the narrow roadway and, ducking down, they hurry along. Both are fearful now. Looking back they realize they have been spotted. They start to run, but the two hooded figures have also got onto the track and are giving chase.

"They're coming after us!" Betty blurts in panic.

"Come on," Dave urgently implores. He clasps Betty's hand, pulling her, helping her to keep up. Glancing furtively back, they become aware that their pursuers are gaining fast. Betty sees something flashing in one of their hands.

"They have a knife!" she gasps in terror.

"We'll fuckin' kill you!" is roared at them from behind.

The pathway twists and turns, but there is no sign of the amusement arcade or the few houses.

"Don't give up," Dave urges frantically.

"It's no use," Betty gasps, faltering.

"Come on, come on," Dave pleads, pulling her hard.

Suddenly two hefty looking joggers come round a bend ahead of them, one a little in front of the other.

"They're attacking us! They're attacking us!" Betty screams.

The two giving chase now turn swiftly and start to retreat fast.

"You dirty bastards!" the first jogger shouts, grabbing up a few fist sized rocks and hurtling them at the fleeing figures. "You scumbags!" he again shouts.

"You fuckin' swine!" the second shouts.

Betty runs to and throws her arms around the second jogger.

One of the hooded men halts and defiantly flings a stone back that whizzes by, hopping off the hard surface. This is answered by a well directed missile which narrowly misses its again fleeing target.

"Thank you, thank you!" Betty cries. "They were after us!"

"It's all right, it's all right," Bill, the second jogger says, giving Betty a comforting hug. Dave has his hands on his knees and is panting breathlessly.

"Are you okay?" Pat, the other man asks.

"Yes," Dave gulps. "Christ, thanks for that. Thanks! You saved our bacon. The bastards were almost on us."

"Okay boy, you're fine now," Pat says, putting a reassuring hand on Dave's shoulder.

Betty, in shock, holds Bill tight. "They meant to kill us," she sobs. "They had a knife."

"Quick, your mobile!" Bill urgently commands, "The guards!"

"Yeh, right," Pat responds, dialling the number. "Are you all right?" he again asks Dave, as he waits for a reply.

"I feel shook. I'm no hero."

"Hallo," Pat speaks on his mobile. "Quick, listen, a young couple were chased and were lucky to escape, here in Curracloe... Bill Fennel... a few minutes ago... that narrow lane through the derelict area... two hooded bastards... they would only for myself and a friend coming along. We were out for a run... yeah, they could be the same two as Courtown... that struck me as well—the same likenesses." He turns to Dave. "You'll wait for the guards?"

Dave nods his head, "Sure."

Pat continues, "Mark the spot. Right... we will... at the car park... okay." He returns the mobile phone to his pocket. "They'll be here as soon as possible."

Dave gives Betty a close hug. She cries a little more, her head on his shoulder.

"It's okay, we're safe now," he says, "we're safe."

Pat extends his hand "I'm Pat, he's Bill."

"Dave and Betty," Dave responds. "We'll be forever grateful to you." They shake hands.

"It was God sent you," Betty murmurs, wiping her eyes.

"We'll head back to the car-park," Pat suggests. "The guards want to speak to us as well."

They start on back.

"I'm still petrified," Betty says, walking close to Bill who puts his arm round her shoulders.

"Don't worry, it's over now—everything is all right," Bill assures her.

Pat loiters back slightly, accompanying Dave.

"It was so quick—out of the blue," Dave relates. "When it happens you're not so brave."

"The two of you hadn't a hope. They're vicious, violent thugs. Something very similar happened in Courtown recently. You heard about that?"

"No?"

"That's surprising. It was big on the papers."

"I don't read the papers much. What happened?"

Pat lowers his voice. "Slow down... I don't want her to hear... a couple like yourselves were hunted down in a lonely spot—they were robbed—the man was kicked and beaten unconscious—the girl was beaten, dragged into the bushes and raped repeatedly."

"Christ!" Dave exclaims, "Only for you then—"

"It was probably the same two. The injured man is still in intensive care." He points back. "Those two bastards would take pleasure in hunting you down—they'd tire you out, terrify you, and then they'd attack. They could have a spot picked out." He waves an arm, "It could even be around here—with that heavy gorse and ferns there

170

for cover. The police will be swarming all over this place soon. They'll get 'em too, don't worry." He again points behind. "They're kinda trapped back there now."

Shortly after reaching the car-park the wailing sirens of the Garda cars can be heard approaching rapidly.

A Man Can Change

Ned Hayes is standing in the lonely kitchen of his farm-house, which is situated down at the end of a long winding laneway, or boreen as it is often called. Ned is fifty-two years old, wiry and sinewy. He has on his strong work-ing clothes and boots, having come in from the yard. He has a cloth cap on his head and is unshaved. He is not unlike numerous bachelors strewn throughout the rural landscape of Ireland.

There is a general air of untidiness about the kitchen. A turf fire is smouldering in the grate, flanked by a battered armchair, with more turf stacked close by. A table with chairs occupies the centre of the room. A few faded pictures and a mirror hang on the walls. There is a Scotch dresser containing a display of cutlery. A cupboard and a television set occupy the left wall. A gas cooker is also in evidence. A strip of wallpaper hangs down from a damp patch on the back wall. A black and white sheepdog is stretched out comfortably in front of the fire. Unwashed chinaware has cluttered up the sink.

Ned has a newspaper spread out on the table and is looking down at it for the tenth time. He has put an adver-tisement in the Lonely Hearts section of a farming paper, which reads:

Lonely farmer, fifty two years old, seeks a soulmate
aged between thirty-five and fifty. Must enjoy country

life and have a GSOH. Social drinker and occasional smoker. Considered handsome. Hobbies: GAA and horse racing. Preferably replies from South Leinster or East Munster. Strictest confidence assured and expected.

He wonders if he should have put down anything about being handsome. It probably looked stupid. *Handsome how are you!* He goes and stands in front of the mirror, takes off his cap and studies his craggy, lined, weather-beaten face. It was brought home to him last week how 'handsome' he was:

Music and dancing had started up in the local village pub. He had asked a couple of young girls out to dance but they only laughed at him. Laughed up in his face. He was conscious of the embarrassment he felt having to walk back across the floor with his tail between his legs. And noticing O'Connor, with his big mouth, grinning at him. Ned observed again his balding pate. He supposed the truth of the matter was that those girls wanted no truck with someone who reminded them of their own father.

It was partly the experience in the pub that prompted Ned to put his request in the newspaper. But then he was reminded of what Jack Freaney said after the funeral, a fortnight ago. Everybody knew that Freaney was a clever man. Marriage came up in the general conversation.

"I'm never getting married," Freaney said. "Those new family laws could trip a man up in a big way. You get married and straight away the wife will own half of everything you have. You'd walk up to the altar, boy, with your whole farm, but when the priest is done with you you'd turn around and walk back down the aisle with half a farm."

Sobering words all right, Ned had thought. *But feck it,*

what does everyone do?

Ned had got a reply to his written request and he had already arranged to meet this lady the following night in Enniscorthy. They spoke over the telephone and agreed to meet in the little secluded lounge of Barrett's public house. This particular lounge was more akin to the old-fashioned 'snug' with the service provided through a hatch.

Now that the time was drawing near, Ned was beginning to feel a little apprehensive, a little nervous, wondering how things will pan out. *Still, she sounded a nice, homely, friendly kind of girl over the phone* he reassured himself. *But then, you never can tell. We should have talked longer,* he concluded. *Anyway, I better go and look at them sheep.* He had lost one yesterday.

It's a long time now since I had a date to meet a girl. He contemplates this truism as he trudges along, his ever-faithful Bran at his heels. The land is on the hilly side, presenting glorious views all around, but at the moment Ned's mind is far from scenery. When he thinks about the fair sex his mind always reverts back to Helen Kiely and to the happiest period of his life when they were walking out together. The wonderful company she was, with that big, warm, welcoming smile. How excited and over-the-moon he felt each time he met her. When he wasn't with her he was thinking about her. They'd go to the pictures or to a dance, it didn't matter.

Then the fatal mistake he made—the one and only occasion when he brought her home to meet his mother. Straight away, his mother made it plain that Helen wasn't welcome. She had no intention of sharing her kitchen with a strange woman from the town. The hurt he felt that day was palpable. Things were never really the same between Ned and Helen afterwards. Nor, for that matter, between

Ned and his mother. Helen possibly saw no future in prospect. Ned had no money to get his own house built, as well as having no security to get a loan. Shortly afterwards Helen emigrated to England. She urged him to join her but, in an anguished state of mind, he felt he couldn't go as he knew his parents would disinherit him if he walked out. He sacrificed the one girl he truly loved for a small hilly farm. It was a decision that haunted him down the years. Later he learned to his grief that Helen wasn't coming back—she had married an Englishman and settled down in Birmingham.

Now, many years later, he is getting ready to meet another woman. Ned goes up to the high field and checks on all the sheep. He then sits down on one of the many rocks protruding above ground. He smokes a cigarette and suffers a bout of coughing. "Those effin' fags are killing me," he splutters. "I must give 'em up—the fags and the booze." He has started to realize that he has a serious problem with the drink. Ned started to drink heavy shortly after losing Helen—anything to try and lessen the suffocating void her departure left.

He gets up and begins retracing his steps back home. He halts at the gateway to the farmyard, urinates against a pier and passes wind loudly, scattering some pigeons from a nearby tree. He stands in the yard, appraising the neglected state of the dilapidated farm buildings and the run-down appearance of the dwelling house. He scratches his head, sighs and mumbles, "Oh God!" He lights up another fag.

In the past he had sometimes fantasized about how wonderful it would be to hear the happy laughter of children as they played around the farmyard and haggard. This was a sound he now felt he was never destined to hear.

The following evening, after shaving—and nipping his chin, due to his shaky hand—he puts on his best Sunday suit, his cream shirt, new boots and cap—fully prepared, he then sets out for Enniscorthy. All the evening he has felt that little tension building up, wondering about what might lie in store. As he drives along he listens to a doctor on the car radio giving a talk about the dangers of being obese. It will be the cause of major health problems in years to come the doctor warns, particularly as regards diabetes. Prostate cancer and other illnesses that men were prone to get worried Ned. He's noticed he's been feeling thirsty and peeing a lot lately. *Anyhow,* he decides, as he contemplates the night ahead, *I'll put all that behind me. I have more on my mind right now. I wonder what will she be like?* He repeats this mantra for the umpteenth time.

Arriving in town, he parks his ten year old Corolla down by the river, close to the hotel. Glancing at his watch he becomes aware that he has a bit of time on his hands. Barrett's pub is across the bridge. The river Slaney is shimmering in the setting sun. Townspeople are strolling about, enjoying the beautiful evening. Enniscorthy is a friendly town. Ned goes in to an off-licence and purchases a naggin bottle of Power's whiskey, stuffing it into his breast pocket.

Passing Kehoe's Bar he decides he'll nip in for a quick one.

Slapping the money down on the counter he addresses Fat Dickie, the barman, "Gimme a half-one, Dickie, for the love of God."

A retired fisherman—a fixture of the place—sitting on a barstool, greets him.

"Hallo there, Ned."

"How are you, Freddie? You're looking well."

"There you are," Fat Dickie says, setting the whiskey down on the counter.

"Thanks." Ned pockets the change.

"Great weather for the farmers," Freddie probes.

"Great for everyone."

"When you see a red sky in the west, the weather is settled," Freddie solemnly pronounces, as if this were a statement of some profound importance.

"You're right, you're right. We could be in for a right spell of weather. We're due one."

"'Twas bad enough for long enough."

"There's a bit of a change forecast," Fat Dickie announces.

"Not at all!" Freddie contradicts him—fishermen are supposed to know those things—"not with that sky." He turns his attention back to Ned. "How are they all in Ardhalagh?"

"Never better," Ned replies.

"That's good, that's good. I wasn't up your way now in a long while. Not since the ould legs came against me—wouldn't be able for them hills any more. But anyhow, tell me this now and tell me no more—did you meet up with the right little woman yet?"

"No, not yet."

"What! You didn't? Be God, that's a holy terror. What am I going to do with you at all, at all? Sure a house is not a home without the little woman. Isn't that right, Dickie?"

"Don't know. I didn't locate one myself yet."

"Oh sure that's right." He scratches his chin. "I wouldn't mind you though—sure you kick with the left foot."

"What are you saying? What did you mean by that?" Fat Dickie angrily demands.

"You know yourself."

"Know what?" Dickie barks. "What are you on about?"

"Nothing, nothing, nothing."

Ned gulps down the whiskey in one movement, not wanting to get involved in conversation—especially the current one.

"I'll be off then. Good-luck."

Freddie is demonstrably aghast at this prospect, after fully and assuredly expecting the offer of a drink. "Heh, hold on!' He stretches out his hand. "Take it easy—what's your hurry?" He hops down off the barstool and almost collapses as his frail legs buckle under him. He grabs hold of the counter. "I have something to tell you," he shouts. "Heh, come back."

But Ned is out the door.

"Feck you!" Freddie shouts. Holding tightly on to the counter, Freddie gazes at the closed door. "That's not like him," he sadly proclaims. "You'd think the divil was on his tail." Turning back to Dickie he thumps the counter with his fist. "I'll tell you wan thing—the days of the ould dacency are gone forever. That's all I have to say."

Red-faced, Fat Dickie still glares at Freddie, who struggles to get back up onto the barstool.

Feeling fortified, and with some trepidation, Ned heads for Barrett's. Frank Barrett is another elderly bachelor who is on friendly terms with Ned. At times, when Ned has had too much to drink, Frank Barrett accommodates him in the spare bedroom at the top of the stairs. Tonight will be one of those nights, Ned decides, as he walks along. He often said to Frank that he'd be fecked altogether if the guards caught him on the road.

*

At this juncture Anna is approaching Enniscorthy from the other direction. She is also feeling anxious, wondering what way the night will develop. It is a complete new experience for her to be meeting a man in this way—or in any way, for that matter. As she rounds a bend in the road and spots the town in the distance she momentarily feels like turning around and driving back home. But that would be too mean a trick to play on any man. No, the die was cast now, there would be no going back.

Ned has a quick chat with Frank Barrett and is told the bed would be available to him at any time. Ned thanks him and takes his drink out to the little-used lounge. The furnishings in this small room are very basic, consisting of a couple of small tables with chairs, soft seating around by the walls, and a few high barstools placed strategically near the serving hatch. Sunken wall lights brighten the room. The entrance is through a dimly lit hallway, leading in from the public bar and the street outside. The service hatch opens and closes and has a small counter to the front. Various posters advertising alcoholic drink hang from the walls. One has a horse sitting in a cart with a muscular man between the shafts pulling.

Sitting down, Ned places his drink on one of the small tables. After a moment or two he stands up and paces the floor, glass in hand, glancing anxiously towards the hallway. Anna finally enters, and excited looking Ned crosses to greet her. He contemplates giving Anna a kiss on the cheek—as he sees on television—but feels too shy and awkward for this.

He stretches out his hand saying, "Hallo... Anna."

"Hallo Ned," Anna responds, shaking his hand.

Anna is wearing a blouse, skirt, jumper, loose jacket

and low-heeled shoes. Her auburn hair is tied back. She hasn't applied any make-up. She is forty four years old. Her clothes appear somewhat dated, giving her an unwarranted staid, matronly appearance. Despite this it is apparent that Anna possesses an underlying attractiveness. She is carrying a large handbag.

"You were able to make it after all," Ned says. "I was… I was getting a bit worried there."

"Sorry I'm a little late. The traffic was heavy."

"It's okay, it's okay." He pulls out a chair. "Here, sit down, sit down. You're right, the bloody traffic is gone to hell altogether. No comfort on the roads anymore. Anyway, you got here in one piece, that's the important thing. And I'm real glad to see you. What will you have to drink?"

"It's all right, I don't drink."

Ned looks somewhat disappointed. "Oh, you don't drink. I see… Sure come on and have something anyhow. Our first time meeting."

"I know… It all feels a little strange. I'll have a bottle of lemonade—or orange, or anything."

"Right. We'll settle on an orange then." He crosses and taps on the service hatch with a coin. It opens, but is not large enough for the bartender to be seen. Lowering his head Ned orders the orange drink as well as another half whiskey for himself. Anna is glancing about as she is not familiar with the interior of public houses.

"Did you have a job finding this place?" Ned turns around and asks.

"No, no, you gave good instructions. Anyway, I know the town fairly well."

The drink is duly served up, which Ned pays for, saying, "Thanks." He crosses and places the mineral in front of Anna. "There you are."

"Thank you."

"Would you like a Kit-Kat or something to go with that?"

"No, I'm fine, this is grand."

"Maybe you don't like the cut of this place? I should have said the hotel above. We could always—"

"No, it's all right." She glances about again. "It's nice and quiet, like you said."

"Yeah, it's quiet all right," Ned says, retrieving his whiskey from the little counter. "Tuesdays and Wednesdays are the quietest days of the week in the pub trade."

"You seem to know a bit about it?"

"You pay well to learn, and I've contributed a fair bit. Be God I have."

"Oh, you have!"

"Well, you know how it is." He sits opposite Anna. "Thanks for coming, anyhow. I was hoping you wouldn't get second thoughts. That's what was running through my head."

"We kind of broke the ice over the phone. I was wondering afterwards should we have talked a little longer."

"That's what I was thinking myself. But what difference!" He clinks his glass against Anna's, toasting. "Good-luck, then. And here's to whatever might lie in store."

"Yes." There is an awkward silence as both are suddenly at a loss for words. "I never did something like this before—made an arrangement like this," Anna says.

"Me neither."

"There's a first time for everything, I suppose… Well, anyhow, here we are."

"Yeh, here we are." Another pause, before Ned blurts out, "At least you didn't turn on your heels and run out the door when you saw me."

"You look exactly as I had you pictured in my mind."

"You look different to what I thought you would— better looking, mind."

"Go on now with your flattery."

"No, I mean it—it's the truth."

"Anyway, none of us fell down with shock, so we'll leave it at that."

"Maybe some people who do this kind of thing exchange photos before they meet. 'Farmer seeks woman with a combine harvester. Please send photo of combine harvester.'"

"Oh I heard that one," Ned smiles. "Not much corn where I come from, so that wouldn't enter into it."

"You're from Ardhallagh, you said. Is that the right pronunciation?"

"That's the place. Close enough to the White Mountain. And you're from Bally— Bally—"

"Ballymacken. It's near Ferns. We're not too far from each other then."

"No. This town would be a kind of halfway house."

"Would you know anyone from up my way?" Anna asks.

"I had deal with a man from the Ferns side once. I'll never forget it. Was there ever anyone belonging to you a cattle-jobber?"

"No, no, not that I know of."

"Good, because this fella was a right whore's ghost." Ned is vehement as he continues. "He took me for a ride, no two ways about it. You see, he had these cattle at the mart that were drugged to keep 'em quiet. When I bought

183

'em I thought they were dead placid—walked up into the truck, no bother. But be the lovin' Harry, when I got 'em home they went stone mad. They'd go for you and that's no lie. They tore across fields, ditches, the river, halfways round the parish. I'll tell you one thing, them cattle will stay with me forever."

"And that man too, I imagine. You couldn't be up to them fellas. They know every trick."

"You can say that again. He had the head of a rogue, so I should have known. A curly head, like a shorthorn bull."

"I dealt with a few of them fellas myself."

"You did?" Ned sounds surprised.

"I had to. I had no choice. A few of them are all right now, to be fair. They helped me out. You see, my father got a stroke and was laid up for years. I was the only one left to look after him. My mother passed away when we were small and my only brother is married and settled in Australia. Doing well for himself, I believe."

"Oh, I see."

"My father died just six months ago. Maybe it's too early to be doing something like this?"

"Not a bit of it. So you're on your own then? All alone?"

"All alone is right. Paul, my brother, had no interest in farming. The land was willed to me. People keep telling me I should sell up and get out. But I don't know. It's my home and what would I do then? I don't know anything else."

"That's it—that's the problem all right," Ned agrees. "You're kind of stuck with it no matter what way you turn."

"It's an awful bloody thing—a stroke. One of the worst complaints there is, I'd say. Getting a heavy man in and out of bed is no joke, I can tell you that. My back was starting to give me no end of trouble."

"It must have been hard going, all right, no two ways about it."

"I knew by the look on his face that it broke his heart what he was putting me through. But sure he couldn't help it—none of us could." She gestures with futility. "That's life, I suppose."

"No let-up at all?"

"Very little. The neighbours were good, but then the place is fairly isolated and people have their own lives to live. Now and then I got a break from it. I used pay a woman to come in and give me a hand to get him on to the wheelchair, and back to bed again at night."

"Your health is your wealth, no matter what way you look at it."

"You can be certain sure of it. And people worry about all kinds of silly things. Anyway, he was my father and he was company. Now that he's gone it's a lonely vigil there on your own. That's why I'm here this evening. Now you know the gist of my story. Tell me a bit about yourself then?"

"Well, to be honest, there's not a hell of a lot to tell. I have only the one sister who is married up in Galway. Ah, she moved up a bit in the world and got high notions about herself. She rarely, if ever, darkens the door now. It's not good enough for her anymore. You know how snobby some people can get—even your own."

"Like myself—only the two of you?"

"That's it. And like yourself again, I live alone as you can gather. It can get you down at times, no doubt about it. A body needs a bit of company, and that's the truth of it. Looking at the four walls! Sure, Christ above, 'tis enough to drive you cracked. You end up talking to yourself and behavin' kind of queer."

"Kind of queer?"

"Ah, you know." Ned dismisses, waving hands.

"Have you a big place?"

"No, it's not that big, but then again, it's not too small—forty three acres."

"That's not too bad. There's only thirty one at home."

"Put 'em together and you'd be going somewhere," Ned enthuses.

"What's the land like? Is it sound?" she inquires.

"Well, a little on the high side. Grazing land, like. It's powerful dry ground for wintering cattle."

"A comfortable house, I suppose?"

"To tell the truth it's not in the best of shape. I'm afraid I left things slide, so it's gone to pot a bit. No use telling you otherwise."

"Maybe it could be worked on—restored back?" Anna suggests.

"It would take time and money—a lot of it."

"At least you're honest about it. That's one trait I admire in people."

"Apart from that, there are no debts hanging over the place. That's one good thing. I pay my way—always have."

"The same here. I hate owing money."

"The car I drive might be ten years old, but it's paid for. That's the way I am. But then, like lots of single men living on their own, maybe I drink a bit too much."

"Could you cut back on it do you think?"

"If I had someone in life, or could see some good reason to cut back, I probably could. I'm sure I could."

"I don't mind a man having the odd drink. But my father, God rest him, always warned me to be careful of

186

any man who drank too much. It was the ruination of too many places, he said. He was able to name several farms that were drank out. The poor wife and children at home hungry, and the husband below in the pub and he not able to put a straight leg under himself."

"That's a common enough story all right."

"Don't get me wrong now—I'm not saying you'd be like that. Sure if you think you can control it."

"When you've only yourself to think about it's easy to let yourself go."

"I suppose it is. Those long winter nights on your own, without a soul to talk to, can be a heavy burden. Especially those nights from mid-November on, when it's dark at half four.

"Another thing," Ned states emphatically, "the countryside is after changing dramatically. There are people going nowadays, girl, who'd slit your throat for money to buy drugs." He realizes he may have made a mistake. "Look, I'm sorry, I don't mean to frighten you. Your house, maybe, is not as isolated as mine."

"I know what you mean. Sometimes, all right, I imagine I hear noises at night. I'd feel frightened, get up, go down to the kitchen and put on the kettle. I could be sitting there at half three in the morning, drinking tea, listening to the wind moaning on the gable-end of the house—like the banshee herself. I think I heard her once too."

"Ah no, I wouldn't say you did now."

"Off in the distance—a weird, wailing sound."

"I thought the electricity got rid of the banshee and the like. What you heard now was an old vixen fox."

"I don't think so."

"You can be sure of it. Or maybe a randy old tomcat

on the prowl—them fellas can sing quare tunes."

Anna sighs, "No matter how you look at it it's hard on a woman, isn't it?"

"It is, it is, in lots of ways."

"For instance, unlike you, I couldn't ramble down to the pub for a drink or a game of cards. Stories would start flying around about me—that easy woman, down the lane."

"Ah no, things are not like that anymore. Attitudes have changed—especially about those kind of things."

"I don't know about that. That's a subject I want to talk to you about. I told you I spent all those years looking after my father—even before that I had led a sheltered life. I never went out much. It means I have no experience of men… if you know what I mean? I don't know like… like how I'd react to a man." Ned looks a bit flustered. "That aspect worries me. How about you?"

"How about me?" Ned's eyes have widened.

"You know. Have you much experience of women? You know… that other part of it?"

Ned gulps at the Guinness, spilling some down his front. "What… what exactly do you mean like?"

"Ned, I have no experience of… of…" She whispers, "of the intimate side of a relationship between a man and a woman."

"To tell you the God's honest truth, I was never intimate with a woman myself either."

"You weren't?"

"Apart from a bit of kissing and cuddling. That's about the size of it."

They look at each other. Anna starts to smile. Ned too.

"I don't know what I'm smiling at," Anna says.

"Maybe it's not the most important thing in the world."

"No, it's not. But listen, we'd want to keep that part of the conversation to ourselves."

"God, we will. Who would we tell it to?" She smiles again. "If you could have seen the look on your face. I think I took you by surprise?"

"You took me a bit off guard all right."

"But what I said was true—I might as well have been brought up in a convent."

"And me in a monastery."

They both start to smile again, their smiles developing into outright laughter at the absurdity of their situation. However, their mutual revelation and the mirth it engendered has defused any lingering reservations between them.

"Anyway," Anna says, "it's nice to be able to talk about things."

"It is, without a doubt."

Ned, in a relaxed frame of mind, is starting to feel guilty about downing whiskey and stout whilst Anna sips at a glass of orange. He suggests that they go for a walk, it being such a nice evening. This is proving something new for him.

They go out and stroll down the street. Ned goes into a sweetshop and purchases two ice-cream cones. They walk across the bridge, turn left and avail of the lengthy walkway down by the glistening river. A sizable number of locals are enjoying this facility also.

An open confession is supposed to be good for the soul. Ned and Anna discuss various episodes of their past lives. Ned says he had gone out with a few girls down the years but the relationships always seemed to fizzle out. He thought better about mentioning Joan Kiely as he felt

189

it might be inappropriate.

A few power-walking, arm swinging, serious looking girls march towards them. They stand one-side to let the determined girls pass by.

Ned loves the soft lilt to Anna's voice. They suddenly realize they have walked a considerable distance and do an about turn. Back close to the town they sit on a bench and watch some graceful swans. Ned brings up the condition of the farmstead again.

"If you put your mind down to it no problem is insurmountable," Anna says.

As the shadow of darkness descends on the town Ned feels a surge of happiness course through him. This was a feeling he hadn't experienced for a long, long time.

Eventually they arrive back to where Anna has parked her car. Ned, anxiously and nervously, asks Anna would she meet him again, "maybe next Friday evening—at this very same spot?"

Anna takes his hand in hers, gives it a tight squeeze and says, "I will, of course."

As he walks back to Barrett's pub there is an extra spring to Ned's step. He feels seven foot tall.

Arriving back he enters the hallway, but doesn't open the door to the public bar as he automatically did heretofore. No, he bounds up the stairs to the bedroom he has become so was familiar with. He becomes aware of the sounds from below—the sudden burst of laughter and the loud voices as some point was debated. It didn't tempt him now. The inner joy to his soul is too profound. He undresses down to his vest and underpants and slips in to bed. He smiles as he thinks of Anna adding that comforting, reassuring 'of course.'

The following morning Frank Barreett is surprised

that Ned hasn't come down for the usual boiled egg, tea and toast breakfast. He goes up to call him, but the bedroom door is open. He goes in and is surprised to see that the bed has been made and the room tidied. He is more surprised still when he spots the fifty euro note on top of the bedside locker and the unopened naggin bottle of Power's whiskey pressing it down.

"Begod," Frank said, rubbing his chin, "that's a big change."